AS MANY SHIPS AS STARS

WEYODI OLDBEAR

ANDROID PRESS

Published by Android Press
Eugene, Oregon
www.android-press.com

Edited by Somto Ihezue and
Justine Norton-Kertson
Cover Art by Sadekaronhes Esquivel

ISBN 978-1958121894

to my children, Weckiai, Wynnona, and Woody,
you give me hope for the future.

CONTENTS

FOREWORD

The stories of Indigenous peoples, my own Ojibwe stories and so many others, are filled with advice about worlds ending and beginning. We have creation stories and flood narratives, chronicles of migration and movement, accounts of ancestors making home in new places and among new people. Some, like those of the Navajo and Quechua, talk very specifically about multiple worlds before this one. The Anishinaabe carry knowledge of star people who came to us in the distant past, and we aren't the only ones. The Dogon, a people in Africa, talk about visitors who came to them from a star now called Sirius C which is not visible to the naked eye, not even with a telescope. It is possible that this star was visible tens of thousands of years ago, but that only adds to the credibility of their oral histories. Another interesting connection between the Anishinaabe and the Dogon is that the Sirius stars, from which the Dogon say their visitors originated, is near the Pleiades, these clusters sitting in relative proximity on opposite sides of Orion's Belt. The Anishinaabe call these seven stars Bugonagiizhig, the hole in the sky, and they are the opening between Earth and the star world.

Threaded throughout all of these stories is the reminder that we are stable when we live in balance with the world around us, and if that becomes impossible then our responsibility is to be ready for whatever comes next. We do this by listening carefully to our stories, to see in them the seeds of our futures and our place in the worlds that may yet be. We select those seeds carefully, plant them in soil made rich by the things we have scavenged or held onto, and nurture them against all hope in a world that sees no value in the dreams that we dream. And when we put our stories together with our dreams, who knows what new things may yet emerge to carry us into worlds unborn.

This is what I love about Weyodi OldBear's story, a story about Comanche who are in desperate need of a future and find it in their horse-stealing past. Comanche who are not afraid of new technology, who know that adapting is a deeply Indigenous thing to do. We adapted to the Ice Age. We adapted again when the great sheets of ice receded. We adapted to new peoples and new animals, developing and modifying all manner of agricultural and technological advances long before Columbus got lost. Indigenous futurisms may have been coined as a term in 2003 by Grace Dillon, a container in which to capture all the ways we imagine ourselves in the past, present, and future, but she is simply describing what we have always done in stories and artwork. Besides, we don't have to imagine a post-apocalyptic landscape. We already live in one.

The challenge for Indigenous readers of science fiction is not only to find ourselves in it, but to find ourselves in it as our authentic selves and not just bit players in somebody else's fantasy of an interstellar manifest destiny. I'll admit that while I savoured Octavia Butler's Parables, this is where I struggled with her vision for the Earthseed religion: that it was humanity's destiny to be among the stars. Apparently she struggled with this too in trying to write a third book, eventually deciding that there was no planet more perfect for us than this one. And of course, we are among the stars right here aren't we. But sometimes survival does look like leaving, and our stories contain that knowledge too, whether we leave by choice or by force, sometimes it really is time to go.

OldBear roots her space-faring Comanche in their authentic selves. Her novel draws on not just only their stories but in history itself. Historically, the Comanche formed as a people and survived by migrating south after splitting from the Shoshone and then welcoming distant relatives, the Náhuatl who were also on the move away from Spanish colonization, into their emergent community. There are later stories about Comanche stealing horses from the Spanish, becoming accomplished riders and traders, incorporating this new technology into their own way of life. OldBear weaves these two parts of her history, migration and horse stealing, into a sprawling story about a people who steal a spaceship in order to ensure themselves a future. Then among the stars, lacking a *place* to root their belonging, these Comanche root themselves in their *stories* and as a result they become more of themselves.

For Indigenous peoples today who are often on the move, often far from home, and often without a place to root themselves in that doesn't already belong to somebody else, OldBear offers something profoundly hopeful. As Taika Waititi comforts his diasporic Jewish and Maori kin in *Thor:Ragnarok*, Asgard is not a place, it is a people. When the ground beneath our feet has been stolen from us, when migration has been forced upon us, our stories are what will root and ground us so that we can stay ready for the worlds that come next. Our stories will tell us who we are and how we can begin again because our stories are filled with such knowledge.

Except Ragnarok is not our story, the land is scarred but not destroyed and she waits for us to return. The land is our ancestor as surely as any of our human ancestors and OldBear does not forget this either. Through our stories we fold time and space, keeping ourselves tethered to a deep past and the land from which we emerged. Even among the stars, it reaches through the hole in the sky and calls us home.

Patty Krawec
Ojibwe Anishinaabe/Ukrainian

ACKNOWLEDGEMENTS

AUTHOR ACKNOWLEDGEMENTS

First I would like to thank my Kaku, my maternal grandmother, for the hours I spent listening to stories as a small child at the Comanche Elderlies Center while she recorded them on her state of the art reel-to-reel tape recorder. Not only did all those hours of listening make me into the storyteller I am today, among those stories was the oral history of how the Quahadi band of Comanches acquired our first horses. That story inspired this futurist retelling.

I would also like to thank my son-in-law, Eli Rannila, for keeping house and doing the unpaid and often invisible labor that makes it possible for me to sit down and write.

Thanks, too, to my son-in-law, Kit West, for our long conversations.

Finally I would like to thank my husband, Robert Watts OldBear for his encouragement, love, and trustworthiness.

ANDROID PRESS LAND ACKNOWLEDGEMENT

About a half hour west of Eugene, Oregon, the Android Press office is located on Kalapuya Ilihi, the traditional Indigenous homeland of the Kalapuya people. Following treaties between 1851 and 1855, Kalapuya people were dispossessed of their Indigenous homeland by the United States government and forcibly removed to the Coast Reservation in Western Oregon. Today, Kalapuya descendants are citizens of the Confederated Tribes of Grand Ronde Community of Oregon and the Confederated Tribes of the Siletz Indians of Oregon, and continue to make important contributions in their communities and across the land now referred to as "Oregon."

We take this opportunity to express our deep respect for all federally recognized Tribal Nations of Oregon including the Burns Paiute Tribe, the Confederated Tribes of the Coos, Lower Umpqua and Siuslaw Indians, the Confederated Tribes of the Grand Ronde Community of Oregon, the Confederated Tribes of Siletz Indians of Oregon, the Confederated Tribes of the Umatilla Indian Reservation, the Confederated Tribes of Warm Springs, the Coquille Indian Tribe, the Cow Creek Band of Umpqua Tribe of Indians, and the Klamath Tribes. We also express our respect for Tribes the federal government still refuses to recognize, and all other displaced Indigenous peoples who call Oregon home.

Want to learn about the Land Back Movement? A great place to start is https://4rsyouth.ca/land-back-what-do-we-mean.

PROLOGUE

Cycle 42,223

22 degrees Celsius

For one long milli-second, Great-Grandpa Whisper had no idea what was happening. A blinding light shot out in all directions, enveloping him. The spray of needles broke through his flesh. The light that surged over him was sharp and piercing, bright white at first, then heating to radiating bands the color of raw meat alternating with chlorophyll green. Great-Grandpa Whisper's ancient gut balked, trying, weakly, to push its contents up his gullet as every neuron in his wrinkled brain caught fire simultaneously. He knew what happened, not just here and now but in all places to all things. For the tiniest gossamer shred of a second, Whisper's mind existed in every place, past and future, where his ancestors or descendants had ever drawn breath from the first lungfish to pull itself onto Earth's rocky shore to the heat death of the universe. For the first time, he saw the small Dark Matter Beings for who they were, and his mind reeled. He was overflowing with cringing horror and boundless joy in full measure, and the whole experience lasted less than a flicker. Great-Grandpa Whisper raised his head and blinked twice, his face full of needles.

PART 1

BUFFALO BUTT: WHO WE ARE IS WHO WE HAVE ALWAYS BEEN

It was 11:00 a.m. and twenty-four degrees, and Leia Wurahapt sat in her dust-covered sedan. She was glad, all things considered, for the dirt. With the dirt from the launch site on her car you couldn't see how old it was.

All she did was turn the key in the ignition. Then she did it again. The engine sputtered once, twice, three times, refusing to start. The choices were flood the engine or give up when the next try would hear the engine roar to life. She tried, then she tried again, and then she closed her eyes and picked her phone up off the dashboard.

"Yeah, Whitman, my car is dead. No, no, it died right outside staging area one. I'm walking over to the launch site now. Give me a couple of minutes. No, no, it isn't going to turn into a problem. Promise," she said, forcing a smile onto her face. The brain unconsciously recognized when a speaker was smiling even when the speaker couldn't be seen. L eia knew that.

Whitman worked Leia's last nerve. She despised him. But then, didn't everyone despise their boss? Everyone Leia knew did.

In the distance, the heat and the dust kicked up the shimmering illusion of small human forms, but all she had to do was blink, and they were gone.

11:58 p.m.
35 Degrees Fahrenheit

Leia Wurahapt was dreaming—dreaming the dream that had worn
ruts in her sleeping brain as deep and dusty as the ones the heavy trucks
had worn from the nearest gravel road to the launch site. The dream
where she was on the bus, standing room only, smelling a bouquet
of other people's body odors and sack lunches, and feeling even more
guilty than usual that she didn't appreciate her life the way she ought
to. It was like a weight, like being pressed under a pile of rocks, until she
couldn't take another breath when she saw him sitting next to the exit
door. Him. Her ex-husband. Her former fellow T.A. The one whose
name she refused to acknowledge after he cut out on her. Not even to
list on the twins' birth certificates.

Maybe, her dream self thought tiredly, she could leave the bus
at the front, near the driver. People didn't like it, and it ruined the
flow for people trying to board, but she refused to acknowledge Mr.
No-Name's existence. She was congratulating herself on her plan
when she spied trouble; there, at the front, the door was surrounded
by the three guys, each one truly messed up in his own way. The
three guys she'd been seeing when she got pregnant with her daughter,
Flower. She hadn't gone through the trouble of figuring out who the
father was. It was more expedient to just cut it off with all of them.
It was simpler that way. Four years later and she still stood by her deci
sion.

Her briefcase, holding nothing but lunch and a midmorning snack
because her work was too classified to bring home, even on a locked
laptop, fell onto the floor.

That was when she realized her mother was driving the bus. Oh.
Fuck. She hated that bitch most of all.

Leia Wurahapt didn't wake up screaming or sit bolt upright in bed. She'd dreamed this dream too many times for that. Instead, she rolled over anxiously, her conscious mind not quite rising to the surface.

2:14 a.m.

38 Degrees Fahrenheit

Leia was snuggled down hard in her bed in a sweaty and now dreamless sleep when she slowly became aware of a ragged beat, like a rattling drum. She sat up. It wasn't ragged at all. It wasn't a drum. Someone was beating on her front door. She looked at the clock. There were two other adults in the house. She wondered why she had to be the one to go to the door, but she knew one was upstairs and couldn't hear the door, and the other, well, the other never woke up for anything.

Whoever it was at the door, if they weren't someone she already liked, and if they weren't bleeding copiously or on fire, she was going to beat their ass.

Leia tried to fight her way out of her pile of blankets, finally compromising and bringing her blanket with her. Whoever it was on the porch just kept on knocking, the two panes of glass at the top of the door rattling.

"Hello?" Leia said.

"Chaz, it's me, Chaz,"

Great. The across-the-alley neighbor. Leia usually felt sorry for him with his confused stare and his fingers burnt black from the crack pipe, but it wasn't usually the middle of the night, and he wasn't usually banging on her front door.

"What do you want, Chaz? It's late,"

"Ummm, sugar, I need to borrow a cup of sugar,"

"Go home, Chaz,

As she walked away, Chaz started banging on the door again, howling, "Sugar! I need SUUUGAAAAR!"

Sleepy determination driving her brain, Leia dragged a chair away from the dining room table and pushed it against the door. Steadying herself against the rattling door, she pressed her face against the two tiny glass panels at the top.

"Don't piss me off, Chaz, if you wake my kids up, so help me I'll…" She couldn't think of anything to threaten him with that was worse than his life right now, so she wedged the back of the chair under the doorknob and went back to bed.

Chaz was still pounding on the door, screaming, "Suuugggaar! Help! Help! I need suuggaaar!" as she drifted back to sleep.

Leia knew without question that the next time she saw Chaz, he'd be sad and ashamed, but not too ashamed to ask for her spare change.

6:32 a.m.

34 Degrees Fahrenheit

Ungrateful was what she was; after all, she could be Chaz, or at least in Chaz's shoes. On the bus for real this time, Leia Wurahapt should have felt grateful for her life.

Once upon a time, her grandma called her "The Great Red Hope," and she was only half-joking. It felt special to be the only Comanche astrophysics major. Even when the white boys who'd been told all their lives they were destined to run everything, were shitty and jealous because she, and to be fair, that one Laguna Pueblo boy, were quicker, smarter, and more consistent.

Pride cometh before the fall. It was one point where her Elders agreed with the missionaries. Pride would bite your ass every time—that and lust. Leia had proven that much to herself, and as was her habit, she liked to go over her work for mistakes whenever she had downtime. Trouble was she wasn't the best at drawing lines of distinction. Work, life, romance, study, family, how was she supposed to scrutinize just one for mistakes and leave the rest of them unexamined? All the so-called stumbling blocks in her life could have happened to anyone, but they hadn't happened to anyone; they had happened to her, the one who was supposed to be better than that. Better than that, but still humble. Better than universal human drives. Better than the random events of the universe. Better, even, than her own ovaries. She wanted to resent all the people who judged her, but how could she, when she came away with the same opinion. She was a mess.

Did her lonely and anxiety-rocked pregnancies make her love her kids any less? She wanted to deny it vehemently, but the truth was she didn't have anything to compare it to, so realistically, she couldn't say. Hell, maybe she loved them more for having had them alone.

Now, Leia was working on what was supposed to be the last best hope for mankind: the colonization of Mars before Earth became completely unlivable. If that wasn't enough to demoralize a person, she didn't know what was.

What was it really like? She did her best to avoid the question because her entire life she'd been accused of being negative whenever she told the truth. If people wouldn't listen to her when it came to the small stuff, how were they going to react to the biggest con of all time?

Still, when had colonization done her, or anyone like her, or anyone she liked for that matter, any good? Not to mention that Mars was a stupid choice for colonization, short on water and oxygen, a narrow habitable zone even after years of unmanned terraforming. The only thing to recommend Mars was its location, and even that was debatable. Even with the best tech available, it was not what any layman she knew would call close.

She rode the bus to work in the dark because her transmission had died, and every dollar she earned was needed in at least a dozen other places, by at least a dozen other people.

She went in, swiped her keycard, said good morning to the only other Natives in the building; also, the only people in the building who didn't get on her nerves, the security guards, Woody, Sarah, and Jerome. Jerome would say something sweet and goofy about his latest conversation with his grandma in Alaska, or his dog, or something deeply thoughtful about art. Sarah would say something insightful or pithy, or both. Woody would nod in her general direction. But even after years in the same workplace, the relationship stopped there, probably because Leia knew she was a wreck, and it made her insecure. She was not about to make the first move for something more and be rejected.

Leia put on her static-dissipative blue lab coat and checked her email. Then, she checked the shelves to make sure all her department projects were on schedule. Next, Leia double-checked the seal tests and the x-rayed parts to make sure no cheap defective components from shady sources had slipped through. She went over her reports. She looked at the x-rays of welds. She looked at fuse tests.

She pulled up her pants, took a break, and made a mug of oatmeal in the breakroom microwave.

What people failed to understand... or maybe that wasn't exactly it. They didn't fail to understand they'd been lied to. But the truth was easy enough to figure out if you went through it logically. The only reason the lie was successful was because people wanted to believe it so badly.

The private project to colonize Mars the whole world was pouring its collective resources into wasn't about saving the human race. It was about saving three shiploads, a head count of roughly nine hundred altogether, of rich people and their families. They weren't heading off to settle Mars for the rest of the species. As soon as lift-off was complete, it was basically "so-long suckers."

Leia and her family being part of the aforementioned suckers, just like everybody else.

And everyone, people in the media and on the street, believed it was this big philanthropic project. Leia didn't know whether to laugh or cry. She wished she could feel smug, but it was no different than her and men. Other people didn't fool you; you could only fool yourself. And only you could sort out the consequences of your own delusions.

What would happen to them when it was over? Leia didn't know. It was up to the leftovers, really. She guessed they would have to take a break from starving and freezing and burning and drowning, not to mention choking to death on toxic fumes and drinking poison water, to solve that one, too.

For the time being, she was making more money than her cousins who were nurses or teachers, or had gone into fast food in high school, and had risen to the lofty rank of manager, though not too much more. Enough that if she stretched, she could take care of some of the people she loved, some of the time. Enough for today.

She had insurance that took about a third of her monthly check, but she and her kids lived outside her tribal service area. Inside her service area, people counted themselves lucky to get minimum wage jobs with no benefits and a boss who thought they owned their time 24/7. plus they got Indian Hospital coverage until the budget was exhausted in June or July. Like the thousands of other Natives whose tribes weren't officially based in Albuquerque, Leia and her family could get basic services from the Indian Hospital System. If they were unlucky enough to suffer anything beyond a head cold or garden variety depression and anxiety and they were at the mercy, or lack thereof, of some local hospital. Never mind the $1,200 taken out of Leia's check every month, her $6,000 per person deductible, and 150 dollar per visit copay. Two weeks ago, the twins, Castor and Pollux, had pushed each other off the monkey bars at school and broken, respectively, their right and left arms, had put her $30,000 deeper in debt. And that was after insurance and after pleading with the hospital's financial services.

Right now, though, she could pay her bills and feed her kids. With the help of her sisters, they could pay their rent. She usually had extra to help family members when they needed it, which was why her car was still parked in the driveway. Someone almost always needed her help. It was a big family.

So what would happen after the ships, stocked full of plants, seeds, and animal embryos, and artificial growth tanks, achieved lift-off was anyone's guess. Until then, she would do what was in front of her to do. It wasn't as if there was any way to simply step off the hamster wheel of bills, routine, and job, and live some other life. Her kids needed food and a place to stay, and there was no way to get those things without money. No way to safely and consistently get money without a job. Having a job meant being controlled by a boss, whether you worked on The Mars Project or the Five Dollar Store.

Her car had broken down four times in the last eight months, and she was working late again. Not that she ought to complain, enough overtime and she could get her car fixed. The bus didn't run out to the research park after 6:00 p.m. She guessed she was calling her sister for a ride. Again.

7:40 p.m.
44 Degrees Fahrenheit

"You're lucky I was at the clinic late; the computer went down, and I had to re-enter my notes. Otherwise, I'd be home with a big bowl, in my sweatpants and no bra," Leia's sister Buttercup said, "and you'd be on the side of the road with your thumb out."

Since noon, the temperature had been dropping from a high of 98. After dark, the research park was half prostitutes and the other half people with no place to live and desperate for some kind of relief, with random hapless fools like Leia thrown in for good measure. The hitchhiking crack was only a joke, but seeing how she paid Buttercup's car insurance last month she didn't think it was all that funny. Not that Leia bothered to dignify it with a response.

"Did you hear about that Sleepy-Eye?" Buttercup said, switching gears with one hand and a Big Gulp between her thighs.

"What Sleepy-Eye?" Leia asked.

"That Sleepy-Eye guy, the one they used to call Cheeto when we were teenagers," Buttercup said. "The hot one. He's superfine like sugar. It's only the dumbest scandal ever."

"That's gotta be pretty dumb," Leia said, rubbing her eyes. She vaguely recalled the name but couldn't pull up a face to go with it.

"Yeah, that girl he's married to got all strung out on pain pills after she hurt her back at the warehouse, started messing around with the boss, ran out on Cheeto, and left him with the kids, one of 'em not even his," Buttercup said, taking a sip on her soda.

Without the soda, she would probably be too tired to drive, but skinny as she was, Buttercup had been playing chicken with diabetes for years. She was probably skinny because her dad had been. That was the way it was. Leia was the fat sister, but she was the healthiest by far.

"Sucks to be him, I guess. I mean, half the women I know have been through something like that. Nobody's lining up to save them." Leia said, trying to sound matter-of-fact instead of bitter. She felt a little bitter, though, since she was one of those women she was talking a bout.

"That's not the worst part," Buttercup said, taking another swig from her Big Gulp and adjusting the picture of her husband, Chuy, dangling from the rearview mirror. Buttercup kept pictures of Chuy everywhere and obsessed over the idea of marrying everyone off to compensate for the fact that the Army had kept Chuy fighting overseas for most of the last decade. He was out on another tour of duty. Leia couldn't even remember where. With any luck, they'd see him again next Christmas. Depending on your definition of luck. Leia was kind of lukewarm on her brother-in-law.

"What's the worst part?" Leia asked, to tell the truth she was a little curious.

"He was working at the language department over in Elgin, but she's the one with all the relatives down at the tribal complex, so when she left him, he got fired. All those kids, and he lost his job," Buttercup said wistfully.

"How many kids does he have?" Leia asked. The way Buttercup said it made it sound like there were eight or nine of them.

"Three, I think," Buttercup said, stopping at the light and hitting her turn signal.

"I've got three kids," Leia said. She would have asked why Buttercup acted like three was a lot when they belonged to a man, but she already knew.

"That's why he came to Albuquerque. He got a job at Southwest Indian Polytechnic Institute. His brother already works there teaching ethnobotany or something like that. So Cheeto's in Albuquerque, he's single, he's enrolled, he's employed," Buttercup said as the turn signal clicked in the dark.

" He's got kids…" Leia said. "But good for him, SIPI's not bad, and anything beats living in Oklahoma."

"Why you gotta be that way?" Buttercup said as she took a left turn.

"I'm not being any kind of way. I'm just saving all my spare sympathy for somebody

special," Leia said in her own defense.

"Who's that?" Buttercup asked.

"Me," Leia answered, deadpan.

Buttercup sucked in her breath as if she was about to upbraid Leia for her mean and scabby ways, but after a pause just big enough to fit a lane change into, they both laughed until Buttercup started to choke on her drink.

8:36 p.m.
30 Degrees Fahrenheit

"We're home from our lives of leisure," Buttercup said, pushing open the door with her phone in one hand and her Big Gulp in the other.

The funny part was that Buttercup was halfway serious about the 'life of leisure" thing.

What money their sister Jasmine made, she made from catering, mostly off the books, mostly for special occasions. So, for obvious reasons, Jasmine was the one who stayed home and cared for all three sisters' kids, saving everyone in the house thousands of dollars a month, while juggling puff pastry and asparagus bisque, and growing the backyard garden. Jasmine also had the size and general look of a twelve-year-old combined with the command presence of a General on the battlefield. Her dad was a little guy from a pueblo on the north end of the state, at least according to their mother. Compared to Jasmine, Leia felt like she was lying on a chaise lounge, having naked men peel her a grape half the time.

Of course both Buttercup and Leia both made more money.

Both were also currently being tackled by their respective kids.

"Don't forget," Jasmine said, laying neat piles of nopales and eggs on the six children's plates lined up on the counter while Leia and Buttercup were busy being hugged aggressively. "Olga's big party is in two weeks, and Tilly's coming into town Saturday. Somebody's got to pick her up at the bus station."

Tilly.

Leia had forgotten all about Tilly.

"Now, help me get these plates to the table," Jasmine said.

Leia moved forward to help, Flower on her hip, the twins' arms still locked around her waist.

Something jumped around the corner from the kitchen to the unlit living room. An automatic, kneejerk-type response would be to call it "dark," but it wasn't so much dark as it was absent. Not there. The shape wasn't there, and neither was anything else. There was a void. A lack. A place you couldn't quite look at because of the sense of utter wrongness roughly the size and shape of a small human.

Leia thought she had something in her eyes. She scrubbed her eyelids like she was rubbing off tar.

"You gotta quit doing that. You're gonna damage your corneas,"

Buttercup said from the other side of the kitchen.

"I got something in my eye; some dust or an eyelash or..." Leia was still rubbing.

"Then use some eye drops," Buttercup said, starting to get annoyed.

"I hate eye drops," Leia reminded her without missing a beat.

"That's because you don't put them in correctly, all you have to do is..."

"Blah Blah Blah blah blah blah," Leia cut her off, working the corners of her eyes now.

When she opened her eyes, whatever wasn't there before had slipped away.

⚓

11:53 a.m.
106 Degrees Fahrenheit

It was hot, but luckily, Leia only had to go across the street.

"I'm gonna take this mess to acquisitions over at Techtopia, Ray," Leia said, not bothering to wait for a response before she stripped off her lab coat and headed out the door.

It only took a couple of minutes to pass through Techtopia's security and on to acquisition's quality control division.

"What's up?" Olga asked.

"These parts. Five hundred forty-two out of fifteen hundred are flawed. You need to go with a new supplier." Leia said.

"Can do. It's messed up that my current supplier would rather make a cheap buck than develop a professional relationship, but there you go. Business is a messed up business. Oh, and I've decided I'm having a Bastille Day Party," Olga said.

"Not the Fourth of July? How patriotic," Leia said.

"Very patriotic, considering if I had a 4th of July Party, I'd be burning the founding fathers in effigy," Olga said.

"Fair enough," Leia admitted. "Anything in particular you want Jasmine to make?"

"Since whatever she makes is bound to be incredible, I'm going to leave that up to her," Olga said.

"Anything else we can bring? Folding chairs? Statue of Liberty. Can-Can girls?" Leia asked.

"All you need to bring is yourselves," Olga said.

"Will my brother be there?" Leia asked. It seemed like an obvious question, Olga being married to Leia's brother.

"I don't know. Ask him yourself. I haven't seen him in ten days, and he's not answering my calls." Olga only seemed a hair more brittle, as the topic of Leia's brother came up.

"I think he's got me blocked," Leia said.

"Me, too, since the last time I called to remind him he has a daughter." Olga said, her grin becoming more forced.

Both Leia and Olga sighed.

"God, my brother," Leia fell short of apologizing for fear that if she started, she'd never stop.

"Yes, your brother," Olga agreed.

"I wish I knew what to do with him," Leia said for the millionth time since Olga and her brother had got together.

"You figure that out, you be sure and let me know." Olga said, her smile finally fading to a frown.

10:36 a.m.
94 Degrees Fahrenheit

The Bus Station. Tilly had told Leia... or if she hadn't told Leia directly, then she'd told Buttercup or, possibly, Jasmine to pick her up at the downtown bus station at 9:30. She'd told somebody. Leia hoped it wasn't one of the kids who took the original message. And she'd texted them from the road, so it was only reasonable to assume she'd be on the bus, but not one of them had caught sight of her yet.

Leia and the twins, not to mention Buttercup and her two, "Alex" Alexandra and "Andy" Andrea, had gotten up early on Saturday morning and driven from one side of town to the other in Jasmine's minivan and were now parked, watching both passengers and luggage tumble off the bus, scuffed up and dehydrated, smelling of exhaust and onion sweat, waiting for that moment when Tilly, tall and long-legged, a hank of long multi-colored hair twisted around her sweaty baby's fist and dark circles around her eyes slouched her way down the bust ramp. But it never happened. Every last rider, young and old, in every conceivable shade of humanity from nicotine sallow to rich Corinthian leather, exited the greyhound, and not one of them was Tilly.

Leia turned to look at Buttercup, only to find Buttercup already looking at her, her drawn-on eyebrows knotted up close together. No, she wasn't looking at Leia; she was looking over her shoulder.

"What the hell?" Buttercup said, only to be interrupted by familiar bubbly laughter in the parking space beside them.

Leia pivoted, wrenching herself in her seat.

There, in a patent leather red convertible wearing sunglasses and lipstick to match, was Tilly. In the backseat, little Daisy was asleep, drooling in identical shades.

"I was wondering when you'd notice me," Tilly said between giggles.

"Where'd that come from?" Leia asked, gesturing with both hands.

"Turns out," Tilly said, taking a swig from her water bottle. "When your ex buys a car using your name, your money, and your social security number because their credit sucks, you get to keep the car. Oh My God, I am starving!"

"Jasmine's making brunch," Buttercup said, sucking her teeth.

Tilly clapped, rubbing her hands together in delight. "What are we waiting for? Let's go eat."

"Follow us," Leia said, turning the key in the ignition.

The digital thermometer on the wall of the bedroom read eight-nine degrees Fahrenheit outdoors and 76 indoors. In the dark, one of the children coughed quietly under their breathing mask. Like good mothers everywhere, Leia, Buttercup, and Jasmine made sure their seals were good, and their hoses unkinked when they put them all to bed. They couldn't do anything about the air quality, but they could do that much.

Down the hall in the living room, the group splurge on burgers and fries long decimated to a pile of greatest wrappers and cups full of ice; Buttercup and Jasmine were sharing a bowl of popcorn on the long couch. On the loveseat, Tilly sat cradling baby Daisy, named for their mutual grandmother, asleep with a nebulizer cupped to her face.

In the center of the room, stretched out on a recliner, her feet raised as far as they would go, was Leia. In her hand, the remote control was getting a workout. The sound was off, but the channels were shuffling as fast as a deck of cards.

"So what are you planning to do, Til?" Leia said.

"Ideally, I'd like to find a job," Tilly said. "Build up some savings, finish my nursing degree if I can."

"In Oklahoma? If you can find a job in Oklahoma, they're going to pay you in loose buttons and pocket lint, if they can get away with it," Leia said, still flipping channels.

Jasmine and Buttercup looked at each other.

"You could always stay here. Pay's better here. More to do," Leia said.

"Not that I can afford it," Tilly said, laughing.

"You could if you lived with us," Leia said. "They're looking for security guards down at the launch site. Think you could pass a background check?"

Jasmine's eyes widened just a little. Buttercup shrugged.

Tilly shrugged, "Honorable discharge. Couple of commendations. No police record. So probably."

"How's your credit?" Leia asked, looking straight ahead.

"Seven hundred thirty," Tilly answered like she kept track. She probably did.

"You'd probably pass," Leia said, unmuting the TV.

On the TV, a white mother stood beside a breakfast table where two children and an adult male were seated.

"I buy Mars Milk for my little guys, but the big guy loves it, too." The TV Mom said, all smiles.

Leia changed the channel, stopping in the middle of another commercial.

Image of "pioneers" slogging through the mud, guiding oxen pulling a covered wagon, then soldiers storming the beach at Normandy, followed by the camera at the base of a spaceship slowly panning upwards, then a close-up of a young Black couple gazing into each other's eyes while pulling off their wedding rings and dropping them in a receptacle mark "gold for Mars."

The voiceover was soothing yet authoritative. "*Together, we tamed a continent and kept the world from the grip of a madman. Today, we're pulling together to build new homes on new worlds.*"

Buttercup and Jasmine looked at each other out of the corners of their eyes.

Leia changed the channel. On the screen, two little white girls in braids ran across an impossibly green lawn, dolls in hand. It was a toy commercial.

The music blared. "*It's Martian Betty, Maaartian Betty, she's out of this world!*"

"What a bunch of crap!" Leia said, flipping the channels so quickly every image was a blur.

"Well, you better believe I've got our lottery tickets. Somebody's got to win, and your baby cousin is planning on bein' the first Comanche transwoman on Mars," Tilly said.

Leia leaned over, nearly tipping out of the recliner to help herself to a handful of Buttercup's popcorn, stuffing it in her mouth and chewing slowly before she spoke, "Baby girl, there's room on those three ships for the richest people in the world and their families. And as soon as they're ready, it's gonna be so-long-suckers. I mean their PR team'll probably hire a couple dozen actors to play lottery winners, but... nobody we know is gonna win. You're gonna be stuck here on Earth with the rest of us."

Tilly turned to face Leia, her feelings hurt. "You don't know that. Not for sure."

"You'll see," Leia said, not looking at anything but the pictures flashing on the screen.

3:23 a.m.
80 Degrees Fahrenheit

It was a bright night in the city, lights bouncing off the low cloud ceiling, and the air hung heavy near the ground.

Leia rolled over in bed, one eye cracked open just enough to focus on her phone. The clock was unreadable without her glasses.

In the distance, she could hear two coughs and a solid hack. She prayed to a god she only believed in when she thought he was out to get her, that it wasn't coming from the kids' room, despite the fact that she knew it was coming from the kids' room.

She pried herself out of bed and trudged heavy-footed down the hall.

Leia bent over her youngest, Flower Array, in the bottom bunk of the corner bed. Her little forehead was sizzling. Behind her, the two other bunk beds with four sleeping/coughing/wheezing children between them, were creaking. She felt the shadow of another woman's silhouette fall over her shoulder. The thermometer on the wall read sixty-eight and falling.

The kids continued to cough.

The twins were sick. Flower was sick. Buttercup's kids; Alex and Andy, were sick. Jasmine's little thoughtful guy Emmet was sick.

Leia wondered if Daisy and Tilly had brought something from Oklahoma.

She looked at the wall read-out and correction: The thermometer reading had fallen to forty-five.

"I'm catering a gallery opening tomorrow," Jasmine said, standing behind her.

Leia inhaled—slowly. She only had a limited number of PTO days, but Jasmine had none. If Jasmine flaked out on a catering gig, not only did she not get paid, she was also out the personal money she spent on ingredients. Plus, there was the slim chance Jasmine might be sued.

"I guess I'm spending the day at the Indian Hospital," Leia said, *but I'll be damned if I'm going alone,* she told herself. "I mean, Daisy is the only one who's not coughing."

Leia marched down the hall and up the stairs to the last bedroom in the farthest corner of the house. Barely visible and wedged against the wall was a figure in the bed swaddled in a pile of blankets untucked from the corner of the mattress.

Leia took a deep breath and...

"Buttercup! Wake up and call in." She didn't quite shout, but she didn't quite not shout, either.

Buttercup didn't sit up or unwrap herself, but she grunted quizzically. Buttercup was the only person Leia knew who could grunt quizzically.

"The kids are sick," Leia said, still in the doorway.

Buttercup sat up in bed, disheveled and bewildered, squinting one eye. Thermometer read forty.

"Our kids are sick, and I loaned that money to Uncle Boy, so my car's not fixed. Not like I could fit all the kids in my car anyway," Leia said. "If you're planning to wake and bake, do it now. I'm not gonna watch all those kids by myself."

"You better see if Tilly and Daisy are okay," Jasmine said, rubbing her eyes.

She checked. Tilly and Daisy were fine, more or less. That is to say Daisy's asthma was the same as it always was.

9:12 a.m.
36 Degrees Fahrenheit

Outside the Albuquerque Indian Hospital, it was raining and 38 degrees. Inside, water was dripping from the ceiling in one corner of the main waiting room into an industrial-sized garbage can.

"I don't so much mind them killing us with substandard care, but do they have to make us wait so long for it?" a man's voice said.

It was an old joke, and Leia didn't care enough to turn around.

"He might be corny, but he's good-lookin'," Buttercup said quietly out of the corner of her mouth, fidgeting with her wedding ring.

Leia Wurahapt adjusted herself in her seat in the IHS Hospital waiting room, Flower and Emmet curled up against her chest, the twins reading with her sister Buttercup's biggest girl, Alex, and every one of them runny-nosed, watery-eyed, fighting random chest-wracking coughs. She listened with one ear for her name on the speaker before she answered him.

"Well, you know what they say, The waiting is the hardest part. Maybe we'll luck out and sit here so long we get well on our own."

"Or die of old age," he said.

Leia turned, nonplussed.

He looked like he should be shirtless on the cover of a hokey greeting card with a buffalo and an eagle made of clouds behind him. Instead, he was wearing a blue flannel shirt and had a baby with a runny nose on his lap, which was worse than posing shirtless as far as Leia was concerned. The only way he could be more appealing would be if he had a pie in the other hand. She turned back, resisting the urge to glance at him again out of the corner of her eye. Nope, the only thing that lay in that direction was madness and possibly another kid. Leia had three kids already so, yeah, she'd met her quota.

"Makes good looking babies, too," Buttercup muttered just for Leia.

"If that's even his kid. For all I know he could have borrowed it from his sister to go babe-hunting," Leia said just as quietly. It was a low-down suspicion, but Leia was well aware there were plenty of low-down, messy, and just plain pathetic men in the world. She had evidence. She didn't produce her kids by parthenogenesis.

"Why you gotta be that way?" Buttercup whispered.

"What way is that? Realistic?" Leia said under her breath. "Besides, the only thing he'd want me for is for someone to watch that cute baby while he's out fooling around with other women. I just finished toilet training Flower a couple of months ago, and I'm not planning on changing another diaper until I have grandkids."

Buttercup sighed but she didn't offer any argument; she probably didn't have the air for it. Andy could barely fit on her mother's lap, but she hung on anyway. As far as Leia was concerned, Buttercup was on thin ice and should drop the topic of conversation. Buttercup was the pretty one—Leia was the one who had looked like a grandmother in the larval stage since she was fourteen: round nose, round belly, round head.

Leia kept her back turned as that baby fussed, and that handsome guy comforted him.

"Kesu, kesu," *slow down, slow down,* someone, it sounded like the handsome guy, said behind her.

"He's Comanche," Buttercup whispered out of the side of her mouth like Leia hadn't heard him for herself.

Of course, he had to be Comanche. Of course a good-looking guy like that couldn't be a member of just any tribe, no, he had to be a member of her tribe.

"Probably has three separate STDs," Leia answered her.

"Man, you must really be liking it for him to bust on him so hard," Buttercup sneered almost under her breath.

Leia didn't say any of the things that crossed her mind.

Of course she was liking it for him.

Member of her tribe? Check.

Spoke his language? Check.

Good Looking? Two checks. Maybe three.

Leia pressed her lips together, hating the guy on general principles. It was like her grandmother had picked him out for her from beyond the grave, including the dumb joke of a name.

No.

Leia's mind tumbled.

No.

A scene from her teenage years came to mind.

The Lawton Oklahoma Indian Hospital elevator. On her way up to the third floor to schedule her gallbladder surgery. Two of the cutest Ndn boys she had ever seen. The elevator clanged and wheezed in a way that usually scared her, but at that moment, she failed to notice because she spent the whole ride up trying to find something to say to them. After all, they were so good-looking, and yes, Leia had always been chubby, but everybody said she had a cute face. She squeezed her brain for something cool and memorable to say to them and came up with nothing in the thirty seconds allotted to her.

Nothing.

And she had just been to the snack bar, so she smelled like onion burgers.

And her legs were so short the back of her pants were ragged from dragging the ground.

She was still trying to think of a way to distinguish herself when the 3 button on the elevator panel lit up, and the bell went "ding," and the doors opened with a grind and a scrape.

Leia still hesitated.

And then, behind her, one of the boys coughed. "Buffalo Butt," he muttered and coughed again.

And Leia stumbled out onto the third floor struggling not to cry.

She had a tough skin, but at thirty-eight, Leia was still bleeding internally from that elevator ride. Nope, she was not interested in anyone with as many checks in his favor as that baby-holder had.

"Han Sleepy-Eye Jr. Han Sleepy-Eye Jr." the nurse called, a folder in her hands.

Leia froze as Mr. Handsome got up to follow the nurse.

"They're calling us, Bubba," he said to the baby, but as he turned, somehow, he saw Leia, and a look of recognition lit his face. "Don't I know you from somewhere?"

"Han Sleepy-Eye Jr." the Nurse repeated irritably and Mr. Hot-Guy followed reluctantly.

Buttercup turned her way, one drawn-on eyebrow arched and a sideways grin crossing her face, and slapped Leia's leg. Hard.

Leia shook her head at her sister.

No.

Han and Leia?

No way was that even possible. It was too spot-on and too unlikely at the same time.

To make it worse, she had the feeling somewhere, her ancestors were having a good laugh at her expense. If Leia had any idea which car was his, she would have gone down into the parking lot and slashed his tires on general principles, not that she did that kind of thing.

Still, it was an exceptional case.

5:20 p.m.
94 Degrees Fahrenheit

That Friday, when Leia got off work, Tilly was waiting for her in the parking lot in her shiny red convertible, sunglasses to protect her eyes, and a scarf to keep her hair from turning into a tangled mess. Buttercup sprawled in the back seat, still in her scrubs.

"I put in thirty applications today, and I swear twenty of 'em were security jobs," Tilly said.

"Just trying to make sure the serfs don't steal the ashtrays before the rich folks run off to loot a new planet," Leia said.

Tilly gave her a prissy, tight-lipped look.

Leia waved away her own comment like waving away a fly. "Don't pay any attention to me. A job is a job right now. Besides, later on, we're going to need all the healthcare workers we can get. All Buttercup knows how to do is talk to people about their feelings."

"Hey," Buttercup said, crunching ice from her soda between her teeth. "Just 'cause I don't use it every day doesn't mean I don't remember my medical training."

Leia looked over at Buttercup with a half-smile. "Mmm hmmm, keep telling yourself that."

"Fuck you too, Leia," Buttercup said, arching one skinny eyebrow.

"Don't take it personal. I'm gonna be worthless, too, after the ships take off," Leia said.

Tilly's phone buzzed loudly. No vibrate. No cutesy ringtone.

"Absolutely," Tilly said. "Yes, ma'am. I'll be there. Non-slip shoes?

No problem."

"What was that?" Buttercup piped up before Leia could.

Tilly carefully laid her phone in the drink well. "I got the job."

"The job at the launch site? No interview?" Leia asked. "No second interview? None of that bullshit?"

"I passed the background check, and that's all that matters, apparently," Tilly said, seeming as stunned as the rest of them.

"Damn," Buttercup said.

"Tell me about it. I start Thursday," Tilly said.

"Two days from now, Thursday? That Thursday?" Buttercup asked.

"Yeah, two days from now, and I'm gonna need some work shoes," Tilly said.

6:04 p.m.
92 Degrees Fahrenheit

Friday, Leia saw Han was in the grocery store.

The produce department if you wanted to be nosy. Han Sr. was pushing a cart. Han Jr. was strapped to his chest. A six-year-old girl was hanging onto the cart, and a toddler girl was in the seat.

"Daddy-daddy-daddy, they have mangos. Can we get mangos?" the oldest girl said, ballet-dancing in a circle around the cart.

Leia turned her head quickly, trying to give herself plausible deniability, but she could still hear him over her shoulder.

"Baby, they're two dollars a piece. We're gonna have to look in the marked down vegetables."

"Mangos are a fruit," the little girl informed him as Leia wondered if it was worth it to switch grocery stores.

She guessed it was one of those things. Once you saw Han Sleepy-Eye one place, you saw him everywhere. Like one of those hidden pictures in a kid's magazine. The hotdog up in the tree would be there forever, and so was Han Sleepy-Eye.

"Could we... could we get... avocados?" Castor said, holding one dented avocado aloft, sniffling. She felt like a bad mother for taking him out before he was one hundred percent well, but the kids got so crabby stuck in the house.

Pollux was standing next to the avocado bin, holding a produce bag expectantly.

"I like avocados," Flower said from her seat in the shopping cart, "and onyungs."

"UN-YUNS, skunk," Castor said, over-enunciating.

"O-N-I-O-N-S," Pollux spelled out letter by letter, one front tooth missing. Leia wondered when Castor would lose his. Any minute now, she expected.

And intruding once again into her peripheral vision was Han Sleepy-Eye with his baby strapped to his chest, a chubby little girl in the seat of the cart, and the other girl still dancing beside the cart.

Leia focused hard on the avocado, trying to plausibly pretend she hadn't noticed him.

"C'mon, Pahtsi, one hand on the cart at all times," Han's voice said as Leia wondered how to make it through the produce aisle without acknowledging him. Maybe he wouldn't notice her. Who was she to him, after all? Nobody.

"Are they cheap enough?" Castor said, waving an avocado at her with another sniff, and his nose rubbed across the other arm, leaving a shiny snail trail. She ought to get onto him, but they'd already used up all the tissues in her pocket, so she chose to ignore it instead. She was a bad mother.

"Here, let me look at them," Leia said, taking the avocado. The price was right enough, but the one in his hand was grayish and dented, and as Castor passed it into her hand, the flesh yielded without any pressure on her part. Rotten. "These are no good, baby."

Castor shook his head.

"Could we have... cauliflower?" Pollux asked.

"Knock yourself out!" Leia said.

"Can I pick one?" Castor asked.

"You know what? They're on sale... you can both pick two," Leia said, feeling magnanimous.

"Two each?" Castor said even as Pollux threw his two in the cart.

"Sure, baby," Leia said.

"Hey!" came a voice behind her. "We gotta stop meeting like this."

All Leia could think was...damn, good-looking as he was, Han Sleepy-Eye was dead corny.

12:18 p.m.
108 Degrees Fahrenheit

As always, it was a perfect sixty-nine degrees inside the lab facility. And as always, Leia was looking for a discreet place to eat alone in the break room. She didn't want to eat with the other electronics-testing monkeys. She had nothing in common with them. Either they had no kids, or they had kids who had affected their lives less than the average dog. None of them lived with their families. None of them gave her any reason to believe they were worried about anything outside the latest game or movie release. She could not imagine an alien more foreign to her than most of her coworkers.

She'd have liked to be invited to sit with Sarah and Jerome, but she hadn't been. She often got the feeling she made them a little uneasy and it was depressing. She didn't like the idea of being lumped in with Whitman and those other assholes, but she wasn't sure what she could do about it.

Tilly was eating with them now.

"Leia, what are you over there for? Come sit with us? What did Jaz pack you?" Tilly called.

Leia sat beside her and unzipped her green lunchbox with the sticker Flower had pressed onto the front. Mickey Mouse. "I don't know. Let's find out."

1:37 p.m.
105 Degrees Fahrenheit

It was a dry and dusty 104.2 degrees at the launch site. At least 104.2 was what Leia's watch said. The dry and dusty part was objectively true. Her newly fixed car was every bit as dirty as it had ever been. Her filter mask was already turning brown. And every little gust of wind brought a new sheet of dust straight into Leia's eyes. She reached under her safety glasses to rub away some of the grit, but succeeded only in driving it into the corners. Her left eye jumped at the sight of some shape that wasn't there. Some line of scampering shapes that disappeared as her eyes began to tear.

Leia tilted her head back to look at the heavy scaffolding supporting the ships under construction. In her lab coat and hard hat, her hair pulled back, holding a clipboard, Leia was making every effort to look professional despite the location. Her supervisor, Whitman, in his jeans and ironic old anti-science t-shirt, had made no such effort. But then he didn't have to.

"Dude, Yurahop, I thought we were screwed when the R316s came in defective, but you pulled our collective nutsack out of the fire on that one. We are ON SCHEDULE," Whitman said.

He always mispronounced her name in new and exciting ways. She'd corrected him the first few days in the lab, but they both rested a little easier when she gave it up as a lost cause.

"I aim to please. Is that why you had me meet you at the launch site instead of the lab?" Leia said, forcing herself to smile.

"Yeah, I thought it was more festive that way. Oh yeah, I'm giving you a promotion… sort of," Whitman lost his jitters after the first sentence. As usual, he seemed aware that she was aware that he was bullshitting her, but as usual, he licked his lips and carried on with the pretense anyway.

"Bill's come down with the shingles. What can I say? Dude's old. So I need you to make sure everything that's supposed to happen… you know… happens. Here and at the lab. Bill's just on medical leave, though, not gone for good, so I can't bump you up a pay grade," Whitman forced a smile but it looked more like a grimace.

"Of course not…" Leia said, agreeing vehemently.

Whitman flinched, and it surprised her. She wondered if he really expected her to argue when it could cost her her job.

"It'll look great when evaluations roll around, though," Whitman said, continuing to cringe as a dust devil danced across the launch site. The air shimmered longer than usual.

"And we'll need to set up a time with Burr to grant you control room access. You're part of Launch Team Purple, at least until dude's shingles chill out."

9:02 a.m.

20 Degrees Fahrenheit

Burr didn't get around to setting up Leia's access until ten days later. Or rather no one told her to show up for her part for another ten days.

Leia sat in front of the camera, trying to have her face mapped for the third time, waiting for the facial recognition software to recognize her.

"Not yet," Burr said from his monitor. "It's like you're invisible."

Leia bent her tongue to the roof of her mouth, willing herself not to crack a smile, not to laugh. That would be considered inappropriate, unprofessional. She knew what the problem was. In fact, she'd run into it at the apartment she'd had before she bought her house. Facial recognition had been designed exclusively on light-skinned people. When confronted with anyone darker than medium pinkish-gray, it simply didn't see them, not that she was going to tell Burr that. No, she'd let him figure it out himself.

Face clenched, Burr pulled out his phone and, Leia assumed, started googling furiously.

"Okay, I think I got it, Wassup," Burr said.

Someday, someone at work was going to get her name right, and Leia was going to die of shock.

"After lunch, when you come in, could you bring in some uuhh make-up... some uuum... no offense... lighter-skinned make-up," Burr said, literally squirming in his office chair.

It was very hard not to laugh.

In the end, it was true; she had to wear white-face to be seen by the facial recognition software.

6:42 p.m.
35 Degrees Fahrenheit

Tony Hillerman Elementary School.

6:30 p.m., she hoped.

Leia's car computer had been fixed, mostly thanks to Tilly's extra money coming in, but the digital clock remained unreliable.

The marquise read "Welcome To Open House Knight," she wasn't sure what was up with that. There were cars spilling out of the parking lot and parked for blocks around the school. Families everywhere. The thermometer read twenty-nine.

Leia was used to being pulled by the twins, that didn't make one holding each hand, pulling in slightly different directions, toward a classroom marked 1st grade, any less painful.

"Come on, Guys, give your poor mama a break," she whined, fully aware she was whining, despite her resolution not to look like the harried single mother, at least in public.

Inside Han was waiting, perched on top of a tiny desk, beaming at her. Thermometer read fifty.

Leia wondered if it was a realistic option to switch schools?

11:02 p.m.
16 Degrees Fahrenheit

Later that evening, Leia sat on the couch, her lap covered with school papers, papers in both hands. Buttercup stood behind the couch, watching her.

"Don't forget, Olga's party's day after tomorrow," Buttercup called behind her as she climbed the stairs to her room.

Leia fought the childish paranoid feeling that she wasn't alone. The silly feeling that in the far corner of the room to her left were two small somethings, watching her and commenting to each other. Leia felt tired and unhinged.

Olga was not one of Leia's sisters, strictly speaking. She wasn't exactly likely to be her sister-in-law much longer, either, strictly speaking, but she would always be Leia's friend. Olga had officially kicked Leia's brother, King, out a few weeks before, so they weren't together anymore, but they hadn't exactly had a chance to get divorced yet.

Or maybe King would come back home, and maybe Olga would let him.

Maybe.

King was pretty good looking, and like a lot of women, Olga was susceptible to that. At least she was susceptible until King took advantage of it too many times or, like King and Leia's, not to mention Jasmine and Buttercup's, mutual mother, his looks faded from too much hard living. It wasn't just his looks, though, Olga loved him, too.

And there was their daughter, Persephone, to think of. Though honestly, Persey might be a good enough reason never to let him come back home again. No little girl needs to grow up wondering if her daddy is going to come home drunk and ranting about the hard, cruel world at 3 a.m. or if he's going to stay out all night... again.

The truth was Leia flat-out liked Olga better than she liked her brother, even before they got together, and she felt a little bad about it. If she was honest with herself, she knew Olga was better off without King. Olga had been Leia's co-worker first. Well, not co-worker exactly. She worked in the lab across the street and did quality control. Every day, more or less, in those early days, Leia ran across the street with parts for testing, and the two of them just naturally got along. More than once, Leia had wished she and Olga had the least amount of romantic interest in women, then all their mutual man problems would be solved.

She wasn't going to let her stupid brother come between them, now.

It wasn't King's fault that out of their mother's four children, he was the only one she never saw fit to dump off on their grandparents. On one hand, Leia knew she and her sisters were better off. She knew their grandparents were loving, strict, and stable, and their mother was as level-headed as a wet cat tied in a sack. It wasn't King's fault he was whiny and irresponsible. However, it was his fault that he never made the effort to grow up and instead cheated on the one woman willing to kill spiders for him, take care of his child, and keep his bills paid.

King was also to blame for taking it as a personal affront that Olga frowned on drunk driving. The dumbass. It wasn't like she cared about him and wanted to save his life or anything.

Her brother was as close to being a complete fool as one human being could be.

Still, Leia knew her brother wasn't a monster. She'd had enough good times with him, and felt close enough to her little brother to feel guilty that she didn't feel more guilty. It wasn't as though she wanted to be mad at him, or that he was likely to do much about his track record of stupid choices any time soon, but still, she felt terrible.

In short, Leia's feelings on the matter were as clear as mud.

She would be happy to go to Olga's party, though she hoped Olga wasn't going to spring a new boyfriend on her yet. Knowing her brother wasn't good enough for her friend wasn't the same as wanting to see him replaced by some random guy. And Olga did seem to choose men at random, possibly with her eyes closed.

9:43 a.m.

88 Degrees Fahrenheit

Leia stood in the breakroom in her blue static-dissipating lab coat, staring at the microwave, waiting for her oatmeal. Countdowns always left her with the same feeling of thrill and dread, even if it was just a cup of mush and not the burn of ignition she was waiting for.

Security Guard-Sarah was across the room with Tilly right beside her, fumbling through the mugs in a way that was downright conspicuous, and Leia wasn't sure whether she was supposed to notice or not. The thermometer on the wall read ninety-three outdoors and a steady sixty-eight inside the lab.

"What's wrong? You okay, Sarah?" she asked.

"I don't know," Sarah said with a cringe that made it clear she knew what was wrong and knew she wasn't okay but wasn't sure it was a good idea to admit it out loud.

Tilly nudged her to speak with the edge of her arm and tilt of her head.

"What's going on?" Leia asked, ignoring her beeping oatmeal.

"I think my check might be messed up. I mean, I looked at it and I printed it out, and I looked at it some more, and it looks like they started taking out insurance. I don't want them to take out insurance. I never signed up for insurance. I can't afford insurance. We go to IHS, " Sarah said.

Leia squinted at Sarah, "I don't want to be nosy or bossy, but do you want me to talk to payroll for you?"

"If you have the time. I went and they told me everything was fine, but I don't think they heard a word I said," Sarah said.

"Yeah, I'll go help you talk to 'em," Leia said.

It took three hours to get it all sorted out, but Leia felt like it was the most satisfying day she'd had at work in months.

7:42 p.m.
92 Fahrenheit

It was a close thing, but all the kids were well in time for Olga's party.

"Thanks for coming," Olga said, gripping Leia's hand in hers. Her happy facade was holding fairly well under the circumstances, but there was a shaky edge to her voice.

"Of course I came," Leia said, squeezing back. "Like I'd let that dumbass come between us."

Olga wrapped both arms around her, enveloping Leia. Leia hugged her back. Normally, Leia wasn't much of a hugger, but for Olga, she made an exception. Her glossy black hair was like an enormous cloud surrounding both of them. It felt good. Not to mention that Olga always smelled delicious. It was all her expensive soaps and lotions. Leia was pretty sure Olga wasn't paid any better than Leia was. Olga was just better at holding onto her money and putting that money to fun uses, mostly because she was better at saying no to other people than Leia would ever be. Leia wondered if it was cultural. Was that something Black women learned that they just didn't teach Comanche women? Nah, it was probably Olga's own personal power.

The power to say no.

"I got you a chair," Olga said, offering Leia a folding pow-wow chair.

"Thank you very much, Madam," Leia said and bowed. They both laughed.

Castor was standing on Pollux's shoulders in front of the fire, both their broken arms waving. Persephone was running with a sparkler, her free hand linked with Flower's.

"If you fall into the fire don't come cryin' to me," Leia said to any of the children who were bothering to listen, opening her folding chair in front of the fire "and you better not burn those jeans. School clothes are expensive."

The thermometer on her watch read thirty-two.

Olga reached out and held her hand. It felt good to have a friend.

Persephone was racing around the yard gobbling like a turkey now, carrying Flower piggyback.

Leia sighed. The chill in the air and the heat of the fire were perfect. Olga had her big speakers on the porch and the bass notes rolled over Leia. The smoke from the fire perfumed the air but stayed out of her eyes. Leia felt perfect, even though she was prepared for it to be a fleeting sensation.

"I fixed you a plate," a voice said at her elbow.

Leia kept staring into the fire, sure that voice was speaking to someone else.

There was a conspicuous throat clearing, and then again, it said, "I fixed you a plate... but if you... you know... don't like onions or cheese, I can fix it again."

Leia looked up. It was Han Sleepy-Eye. All six foot something, beige and neatly dressed inch of him. Han Fucking Sleepy-Eye. And a traditional, old time, and, most importantly, public come-on. Golden fry bread, beans, ground beef, fresh salsa, lettuce, cheese, and onions stacked up carefully on a plate, a red Solo cup in the other hand.

She looked back over at Olga. Olga dropped her hand and nudged her, whispering out of the corner of her mouth, "Go on, take it. Are you nuts, Lay?"

Reluctantly struggling with the twin giants known as pride and defensiveness, Leia turned her face from Olga to Han.

"Did you get me a drink?" She asked him.

"Dr. Pepper," he said, the confidence draining from his voice. Most Natives Leia knew drank Pepsi. Leia didn't know why it was a thing, but it was a thing. Maybe it had something to do with the lack of safe drinking water across Indian Country. Leia, however, preferred Dr. Pepper on the rare occasion she had soda. She'd always been a weirdo. She guessed Han could tell.

Leia shrugged, "Okay," she said, taking the plate and the cup.

It was probably the Dr. Pepper that did it.

For the rest of her life, Leia would claim not to remember exactly how what happened later... happened. That was mostly true. She didn't remember who started it. She normally hated when men made the first move, but Han was so damn forward, it might have been him. Ma ybe.

With the two of them, anything was possible.

What she did remember wasn't fit to tell anyone but Olga.

She remembered Han's younger two kids, Jr. and Thuni, asleep in a pile on Olga's couch with Flower wedged between them. She and Han shut the door, terrified of waking them.

The thermometer on the living room wall read 99. Maybe it was broken.

What she did remember very clearly was Han's lips fastened to the crook of her neck. The tiny hairs on her arms were standing at attention as she opened the door to Olga's spare room and found it was occupied only by coats. She remembered the excited fumbling followed by sixty full seconds of trembling she was unable to stop or even slow down. She remembered Han's hand over her mouth, trying to keep her from waking the kids as she sunk her teeth in his fingers.

She remembered watching Han naked and asleep under a pile of coats while she pulled up her jeans.

She remembered thinking he needed to work on his stamina. The thermometer on her watch read seventy-two.

She remembered flashing police lights in front of the trailer, beside that, getting a little sex seemed pretty trivial.

Leia forgot about her shoes. Leaving the screen door flapping, she rushed out to Olga, where she saw her face-to-face with two cops.

Leia was prepared to ask them why they were here, where their warrant was, the whole spiel when....

"Ma'am," one of the cops said.

"It's okay," Olga said, locking her left arm with Leia's right, "She's his sister."

"My condolences," the cop said, "Would you like to ride along? Or we can do this down at the morgue in the morning."

Olga made a tiny squeak in the back of her throat, then whispered, "What do you think, Lay-lay? I don't know if I can do it on my own."

"What happened?" Leia asked.

"Your brother, Mr. Frank King..."

"King Frank, you mean, people always get that backwards,"

"That's right, excuse me, King Frank ran his truck into the Rio Grande..."

"He's dead?" Leia asked, everything around her suddenly seeming very real.

"Yes, ma'am," the cop said matter-of-factly, "We believe so, Ma'am. The truck is registered to Missus Frank, but we're going to need someone to make a positive identification of the body. It can wait until the morning if you like."

At her shoulder, Leia could hear Olga breathing fast and shallow.

"What am I going to say to Persey?" Olga murmured.

And it occurred to Leia that she didn't want to ask if King had drowned, not in front of Olga, but if he had, she didn't want to wait until the morning to see him. She didn't want to see him damaged or ugly. She didn't want to see him at all. Not really. She wanted to pretend he was off with some woman, so she could be pissed off rather than heartbroken. Did she feel heartbroken or even sad? Leia checked her head and body for response to the news that her only brother was dead. Probably dead. Might be dead. She wouldn't know for sure until she saw him so she guessed her body was holding back its reaction until things were more definite.

"Why don't you stay here, and I'll go with them, O," Leia said.

"Would you?" Olga squeezed Leia tight, "Thank you, Lay-Lay, thank you," Olga whispered, her hot tears soaking into Leia's shoulder.

10:30 p.m.
70 Degrees Fahrenheit

Leia walked in a daze and sat herself in the back of the police car.

"Are you sure you want to do this now? It can wait until the morning," the cop asked.

"Yeah, I know. I'd just as soon get it over with than stay up all night wondering," Leia answered.

It wasn't until a minute or two later, when they were headed down the highway, that she realized she was barefoot, with a piece of green glass embedded in the ball of her foot. And she should have told someone to take care of Olga before she left. Someone needed to take care of Olga.

11:12 p.m.
52 Degrees Fahrenheit

King's pick-up was still wet and on the back of a tow truck when she got there. The passenger side was more or less crushed in. Both King and someone else were in the back of an ambulance. Although the other body was covered with a sheet, long blonde hair peeked out from the edges of the cloth. Leia was glad Olga didn't have to see that. It was typical of her brother, though, not to go down without taking someone else with him.

"For the record, is that the body of your brother? Mr. Frank King?" cop number one asked.

Leia looked at her brother. The body of her brother. Aside from being wet and having had his clothes cut off of him by paramedics, King looked more or less like an ashy gray, rubbery version of himself. Leia couldn't see any sign of injury. He also, in some way Leia couldn't quite put her finger on, reminded her of a plucked chicken.

"King Frank," Leia said. "That's him, alright."

She expected to feel something, but she didn't. Her bare bleeding foot had left a trail across the asphalt. A drop of rain hit her face, then another. She looked down. Tiny bits of sleet were bouncing off the asphalt. She checked her watch. By the river, it was thirty degrees. It was 12:02 a.m.

1:17 a.m.
70 Degrees Fahrenheit

When the cops brought her back to Olga's house, the black night passing by without stars, only sleet, everyone was gone.

"Where is everybody?" Leia asked.

Olga sat at the kitchen table, her elbows on the table, her eyes on fire, her eyebrows pushed in five or six different directions.

"I told them to go home. Flower's asleep with Persey. Jasmine and Buttercup took the twins with them. Was it him?"

Leia nodded.

"Was he alone?" Olga asked, and Leia wished she hadn't, but Olga wasn't stupid.

Leia shook her head.

Olga couldn't hold back anymore. She pursed her lips tight trying to hold in, and her shoulders fell, then rose, and a sob escaped, then another. In a matter of seconds, she was bawling.

That son-of-a-bitch, that stupid irresponsible shitty son-of-a-bitch. He didn't deserve those kind of tears. Leia reached out and held Olga's hand as she cried. Leia wondered why she wasn't crying, too.

After a few minutes, Olga snuffled, wiping her eyes on the back of a well-manicured hand.

"Would you get me the tissues?"

"Of course," Leia said. She knew exactly where Olga kept the tissues. In the living room, beside the couch, on an end table, under a tissue box cover her grandma had made when they were in high school.

"Oh, Lay-Lay, you're bleeding," Olga said, then paused, a little confused. "Did you go with the police barefoot? Why were you barefoot?"

Leia shrugged, unable, or perhaps unwilling, to explain about Han Sleepy-Eye after the night they'd had. It seemed so pointless and foolish. She couldn't help herself, she laughed.

She was relieved when Olga laughed, too.

Sometimes, particularly in the worst of times, that seemed like all you could do.

9:02 a.m.
92 Degrees Fahrenheit

Leia woke up on Olga's couch, which she had to admit was more comfortable than her own bed, the air conditioner blasting. Olga was on the phone. It sounded official.

"Last four... 9... 1... 4... 5," Olga said slowly and carefully, enunciating like she was speaking to a bureaucrat. "Will I be able to sign that virtually, or do I need to go down to the morgue?"

Leia tried to keep her eyes closed, but it was no good, she wasn't going back to sleep.

"Is there anything else I'll need to make sure everything goes through?" Olga asked in a voice that was pleasant and alert. A fake smile shaped itself around the words coming out of her mouth, but the rest of her was still in her clothes from the night before, still smelling of the fire pit, and her eyes were dressed in a web of red blood vessels.

"Thank you for your assistance, Carol," she lied.

"What was all that about?" Leia asked, propping her aching head in her hand.

"Well," Olga sighed with the weight of the last twelve hours in a single breath, "The tribe will pay to ship his body to Oklahoma and bury him there, but they won't even pay for a cremation in New Mexico."

"I'm sure we could all chip in, and it would cost less than going to Oklahoma ..."

"We're going to bury him in Oklahoma. It's what he wanted," Olga said. "He wanted to be buried with the rest of your family in the Comanche section at Highland Cemetery."

"By all means, let's make sure King gets everything he wants," Leia said.

"I talked to Jazz and Buttercup and they agree with me," Olga said.

"Do whatever you want to do. Do whatever you think is right," Leia said, covering her eyes with her arm. She hadn't had a drop to drink, but she still felt painfully hungover.

"Lay-Lay..." Olga said, sounding sad and frustrated. "I'm sure you can get off work, he's your brother."

"I'm sure they'd let me off, too, if I asked for it," Leia said. "But I'm not going to Oklahoma. Because I don't want to see my mother. I'm not gonna go watch her cry crocodile tears and tell me how much she loves me while she talks shit behind my back about what a shitty person I am and figures out how to get all the money she can out of me "

"It's supposed to be about King," Olga said.

"But it's not gonna be," Leia said. "As soon as my mother's there, it's all gonna be about her and how pathetic and lost she is without her precious baby boy. Well, I don't want any part of that, and I don't want my kids to be around her."

"I can't do this by myself," Olga said, her voice small, squeezing Leia's guts like a fist.

"You talked to Jasmine and Buttercup already, what did they say?" Leia asked, not sure what she was hoping to hear.

"They're coming," Olga said, her voice soft, threatening to break or turn into a whisper, one or the other, "but I was hoping you'd come, t oo."

"I love you, Olga, you know that, right?" Leia said.

"I know, Lay-Lay," Olga said, nodding small.

"I'm sorry, I can't... no, I," Leia shook her head. She was a shitty friend and a shitty sister, but she literally could not bear the thought of seeing her mother. "I won't give my mother the opportunity to hurt me any more than she already has. I'm just not willing."

"I love you, too, Lay," Olga said as Leia jumped to her feet. "Where are you going?"

"Sorry, O, I've had to piss since I woke up. My bladder is about to explode," Leia said as she high-tailed it to the bathroom. In the bathroom, she stared in the mirror and waited to cry, but nothing happened. Absolutely nothing. She wondered if she was a monster.

10:34 p.m.
98 Degrees Fahrenheit

When Leia got home, Flower sleeping hard in her arms, drool pooling on Leia's shoulder, both Jasmine and Buttercup were packing themselves and their kids to go to Oklahoma.

"Olga says you aren't going," Buttercup called from her room.

"Why should I?" Leia asked, "Can you think of a single good reason why I ought to go?"

"Jesus Christ, He's your own brother, Leia," Jasmine called from her room.

Leia was prepared for the argument and fully expected to feel anger rising in her gullet, but to her surprise, she felt nothing. "I'm not giving that woman another chance to mess with me... besides, I kinda think King's past caring, know what I mean?"

Buttercup stared hard into the thirty some odd year-old suitcase she'd inherited from their grandparents. Leia wondered if she had a movie playing on her phone in there. Leia peered over her shoulder just in case, but no such luck. No movie, just resentment.

Buttercup turned around. "You know what? Don't talk to me. I don't want to talk to you anymore. I'm tired of talking to you."

Leia wanted to laugh. Buttercup was tired? She wondered why she held back so much. She felt like laughing so she ought to laugh. It was fucking ridiculous. Buttercup was tired? Leia repositioned Flower on her hip and laughed out loud. It felt forced and sounded loud even to Leia but she laughed.

Jasmine immediately stuck her head inside the door. "Everyone's emotions are running high right now..."

"I'm feeling surprisingly calm right now to tell the truth," Leia said following Jasmine out into the hall. "I'm not sure what I'll do about the kids while you're gone but I'll figure it out. I'm a very resourceful person."

Flower was a big girl and already starting to slide down Leia's hip again. Leia lumbered toward her room only to find her bed already occupied by Daisy, wearing her mother's sunglasses and bouncing up and down on her mother's back.

"You hear all that?" Leia asked, easing Flower down on the bed next to Tilly.

"Your house is big, but it's not that big," Tilly said half shrugging as she rubbed the sleep from her eyes.

"I don't know what the hell I'm gonna do," Leia said.

"We're gonna do, you mean. I wonder if maybe Sarah's grandma can watch the girls for us, get the twins to school and pick 'em up? She already takes Milton, Sarah's five year old." Tilly offered.

"You think she'd do it? Is she up to it? That's a lot of kids even if it's just a couple of days," Leia said, knowing in her heart it was too much to ask from anyone, much less someone she'd never met.

"The worst she can do is say no, which won't be any different than not asking. Besides, we could always offer her money," Tilly said, picking up Daisy by the belly and flying her over the bed.

Leia opened one eye. "You sure? You could always go with them to the funeral if you want."

Tilly opened her eyes brightly, turning to face Leia full on. "I'm not trying to be ugly but the only time your brother had anything to say to me it was to call me a faggot. It's not like it's great to be trans in Oklahoma even if it's just to visit."

"Thanks, you know, Tilly, I appreciate having you here. I like having you around," Leia said cuddling up next to Flower and drifting off to sleep.

12:22 a.m.
42 Degrees Fahrenheit

Never in her life had Leia been one of those people who were prone to insomnia. She was not the type to lay in bed and pore over her day's, or life's for that matter, mistakes. Why wait until the last minute? No, Leia went over every misstep all day long, usually while other people were talking. She was completely worn out by the time she went to bed and dead to the world within sixty seconds of her head hitting the p illow.

The night her sisters and their assorted kids left for King's funeral in Oklahoma, Leia lay in her bed, the mask of her breathing machine strapped firmly to her face and her thoughts ricocheting around inside her skull like a rubber ball trapped inside a bouncy castle.

How long were her sisters going to be mad at her? Were they still going to be angry when they came back? Would they move out when they came back? Both of them or just Buttercup? If Buttercup left, how would they make the mortgage? If her credit was wrecked by losing the house, would she be able to find a rental? Should she even be worrying about it at this point? Did she have more right to be angry at them than they had to be angry at her? Had she even done anything wrong? Was she a bad sister for not knowing the answer? Was she a bad daughter? Did she have it all wrong? Did she, in fact, owe it to her mother to put up with an indefinite amount of verbal and financial abuse as well as endless badmouthing behind her back? Her mother's badmouthing always consisted of the truth twisted until it was almost, but not quite, a lie. Did that make it the truth? Maybe Jasmine and Buttercup were already over it and had sent her a friendly text to make up.

Leia fumbled for her phone in the dark, hoping against reason and experience that Jasmine, at least, had texted. The phone slipped out of her hand and skidded across the carpet. She couldn't reach it without taking off her mask.

There was only one text on her phone that wasn't work or spam. It wasn't from Jasmine though, it was from Han.

I'm sorry for your loss. Drop by ANY TIME. 4444 Brilliant Way.

She could only assume that was his address.

A few minutes later, on her way out the door, Leia passed by Tilly watching an infomercial on broadcast TV on the couch, eating leftovers out of a plastic container.

Tilly saluted as Leia lingered guiltily.

Leia saluted right back.

"Wrong hand," Tilly said.

Leia shrugged. She'd completely forgotten that Tilly did a stint in the army.

1:36 a.m.

38 Degrees Fahrenheit

When Leia got to Han's house, he was sitting on the porch like he knew she was going to show up.

Leia hated that, but not enough to turn around and go home to lie in bed at the mercy of her own brain.

An hour later, she was standing in his bedroom, trying to get the twist out of her bra without taking it off again, when she said the words that had been forming in her brain all evening.

"I don't want to give you the wrong impression. I don't know what you think this is," Leia said, finally giving up and unhooking her bra so she could undo the twist. "I'm not looking for a dad for my kids. I'm not... I just want you to understand now... we're not... we're just..."

"Yoko hytes," Han said, still naked, still in bed, his head tilted sexily.

"Yeah, yoko hytes," Leia nodded. She hadn't heard that phrase in years, but then she hadn't had sex with a Comanche man since she was a teenager.

Han shrugged. "Being fuck buddies doesn't mean you can't hang out and watch a little T.V., does it?"

"Got any good snacks?" Leia asked.

"I can make nachos," Han said, "I make a mean nachos."

"Yeah, I guess," Leia relented. She liked nachos. And sex.

So she sat with Han in his dark bedroom, eating nachos and watching ancient black and white reruns on local broadcast TV. The thermometer read thirty-six.

Then the commercials came on.

The announcer's voice was deep and authoritative, yet calculated to be comforting.

And while the whole world waits, work continues.

"Turn that shit off," Leia said, her patience snapping.

Han turned, looking closely at her face in the darkened room.

"I thought you worked for the Mars Project," Han said.

"Yes, I do. You're very smart. You don't miss a thing, do you? Now will you please change the channel?" Leia said too exhausted to explain anything.

Something unknown watched in the corner.

6:49 a.m.
40 Degrees Fahrenheit

Two weeks later, Leia was met outside the front door of the lab by Sarah, looking like she was trying to swallow a mouth full of wasps.

"What's wrong?" Leia asked, both pleased and distressed that this time Sarah had come to her without Tilly pushing her. It must be pretty bad.

"They left my overtime off my check again. I swear they're trying to get rid of me because I'm pregnant," Sarah said, biting the inside of her cheek and rolling her eyes upwards, trying not to cry.

"What a bunch of bullshit. We're gonna see about this," Leia said, not bothering to take off her backpack as she stomped her way in the general direction of payroll.

"Tell me about it, it's not like they aren't already taking the best of everything. Could they at least pay me for watching them steal it," Sarah said, her voice threatening to break as she followed along.

"I can't do much about the stealing, but at least I can straighten out this shit," Leia said, shifting her face into a big fake smile as she opened the door to the payroll department.

7:34 p.m.
70 Degrees Fahrenheit

Three days later, Leia saw Han again, but not intentionally. All she did was turn the aisle in the grocery store, and there he was, Han Sleepy-Eye. All his kids were with him, as usual. He was standing beside a pyramid of onions, waving his arms like a windmill.

Leia waved back as small as she could. Grateful that at least she was by herself.

Late that night, her sisters and their kids came home. Every one of them, Leia included, pretended that they hadn't just driven over a thousand miles round trip to bury their only brother.

The thermometer read thirty-two.

12:10 p.m.
97 Degrees Fahrenheit

The next day, five minutes before Leia's lunch break, she came in from her lab across the street with a tray full of parts back from testing.

"Well, I'm back," Olga said before Leia could say a word.

"How was it?" Leia asked.

"More or less what you'd expect."

"Was it before or after the funeral that my mother took Jasmine and Buttercup out to smoke pot and talk shit about me?" Leia asked.

"After," Olga laughed a little bitter half-laugh, eyes focused on the parts in front of her. "If it's any consolation, Jasmine says your mom talked almost as bad about me as she did about you. According to her, I'm responsible for King's accident."

"What kind of mental gymnastics did she use to justify that?" Leia asked, dreading the answer.

"Oh, I'm controlling, I never understood him, that kind of thing," Olga said breezily, like it wasn't tearing her up inside.

"So you not wanting him to drink and drive and screw around with other women caused him to drink and drive and screw around with other women?" Leia squinted at Olga's downturned face.

"Respectfully... fuck your mother," Olga said, lifting her head to look Leia in the eye, and it was delightful.

"Yeah, fuck my mother... Your parts are x-rayed," Leia extended the tray to Olga.

"Thank you, I need those things. Did they pass inspection?" Olga was all business again.

"Surprisingly, yes, there's a 100% pass rate for this lot," Leia said, and her stomach made a noise. "Is it your lunch break yet? We could be irresponsible and go get ice cream for lunch," it was more a plea than a suggestion on Leia's part.

"That sounds like the best bad idea I've heard in a long time," Olga agreed.

The thermometer read one hundred and seven by the time they got back to their respective labs.

11:02 p.m.
22 Degrees Fahrenheit

That night, Leia was drifting off to sleep—her mask strapped to her face, bite-guard in place to keep her from doing damage to her back teeth—when her phone made a noise like a rattlesnake. It was a text. From Han.

What are you doing? He wanted to know.

Not much, she answered, *How about you?*

Standing on your porch, trying not to freeze to death.

Leia practically fell out of bed, dropping her phone in the sheets.

When she picked it up again, the thermometer read nineteen. She put on her robe and slippers and spat out her guard before she went to get rid of him.

"I figure you've been busy, or you woulda called," Han said, stamping his feet to stay warm.

"Yeah, I work a lot. Listen, I don't have men at my house. It's a rule. I don't want strangers around my kids," she said.

"But if they get to know me I won't be a stranger," Han said.

Leia chose not to dignify that bullshit with an answer.

"My kids are asleep. Your sisters are home. You could come over to my place," Han said.

"Like this?" Leia whispered. Her hair was in two braids, and she was wearing a t-shirt and gym shorts. Her slippers were a pair of fuzzy bear paws.

"You look good to me," Han said. "Pleease? I promise I'll get you back before your kids wake up."

"I can drive myself," Leia assured him.

4:13 a.m.
18 Degrees Fahrenheit

Leia's brain snapped awake. Beside her, Han was naked, asleep, barely covered by a strategic sheet. Leia wiped herself with the other end of said sheet and fumbled out of bed to get dressed, if a t-shirt and shorts could be considered dressed. Her hair was still technically braided, but those braids, man... frayed was an understatement.

If asked to explain what she was doing with Han Sleepy-eye, Leia would be forced to say hope springs eternal from the human heart, but she didn't think that was the organ that was motivating her.

6:33 a.m.
75 Degrees Fahrenheit

Leia did her level best to keep things as inconspicuous as possible. She poured herself full of coffee, showered, kissed her kids, and went to wo rk.

She had oatmeal from a mug in the break room with Sarah. The thermometer read 68.

She had supper at the supper table with her family; sisters, kids, sisters' kids, the usual suspects. The thermometer read seventy-eight.

11:06 p.m.
22 Degrees Fahrenheit

Two nights later, she was sneaking out of the house when she felt a tug on the back of her shirt. There, behind her, was Flower in her PJs.

"Where you goin', Mama?"

"Oh, nowhere, just checking the mail," Leia lied.

"When you come back in will you cuddle me a little bit?" Flower asked.

Leia fingered her phone inside her coat pocket. Standing at the curb pretending to look in the mailbox she texted Han.

Change of plans. Not going to make it tonight. My kid needs me.- L

Han answered her with three thumbs up. She guessed it was supposed to mean he understood and approved. Not that she cared what he thought.

The next night, Leia fell exhausted on Han's bed. The clock read 12:31 a.m. The thermometer read ninety-two.

"Is this the part where you tell me we've got to stop meeting like this?" Han asked, sitting with his legs folded in his own lap. Leia wondered if he did yoga, but she didn't want to pry.

"No, this is the part where I ask for a foot massage and a beer," Leia answered.

"I've got Dr. Pepper," Han said, his arms spread.

"Close enough," Leia was willing to compromise

"I don't drink alcohol," Han said with the earnest tone of someone who thought no one else should either.

"Good for you," Leia said, hoping he wasn't trying to have a conversation with her.

9:01 a.m.
55 Degrees Fahrenheit

Leia was simultaneously bone-tired, contented, and terrified, trying not to fall asleep in her oatmeal.

"I hear you guys are gonna be done ahead of schedule," Sarah said nervously.

"Miracle of Miracles, right? Not much left to do but triple check the triple checks while the biologists fill the biome manifests," Leia said, shoveling oatmeal into her mouth and resenting a freeze dried berry for having both the flavor and texture of a rock. "But our launch date's not going to change. It would be more expensive to change the launch than it would be to pay all the employees for a couple of extra weeks."

"What are we gonna do after? Any idea?" Sarah asked, her thumb twisted in the corner of her giant security uniform top.

Jerome hadn't said a word, but instead was plowing his way through two giant homemade subs. It was, strictly speaking, his lunch break.

"No clue," Leia said, wondering if anyone would notice if the big coffeemaker disappeared after launch.

Kkkkrrrreeebubububu!

Leia looked up to the sound of a chair being dragged toward them from another table. It was Woody. He raised his chin in her general direction, which was a lot more acknowledgement than he ever gave Whitman. Tilly was behind him with her own chair.

"Go on, don't stop on her account, I promise Leia will not turn you in for disloyalty," Tilly said, plopping herself down next to Woody. "You should hear the things she says at home."

Woody cast his eyes around the room. Leia was the only engineer present. It wasn't official in any way but all the other engineers ate, took their breaks, and drank their coffee in the smaller, better-equipped break room on the other side of the facility.

"I'm not trying to hurt anyone's feelings, I'm just saying it's not for me," Woody said as if making a formal announcement.

Leia's face must have asked the question for her.

"It's space," Sarah answered the question anyway. "Woody hates space."

"I don't hate space," Woody repeated. "I just know it's not for me."

"I don't care. I still think space is keen," Jerome said, finally pausing between bites to contribute to the conversation.

Woody, small and wiry, leaned over his company-provided cup of coffee. "I just mean the Earth is our relative, literally. Every molecule in our bodies originated where? Earth. We evolved on Earth. We designed ourselves to live on Earth. Every living thing on Earth is related to us Human Beings. Why the hell would we want to leave?" Woody didn't make a move as he spoke and was all the more intense for it.

"Aside from it becoming uninhabitable, you mean?" Sarah said between sips of water.

Everyone looked at Leia expectantly. Maybe they thought she was going to be offended.

All she could come up with was, "Everything you've said is true."

"But?" Woody said, prepared for some contradiction, his hands pressed down flat to the table.

"No buts," Leia said, putting a spoonful of bad oatmeal in her mouth and swallowing before she went on. "And Mars in particular is a bad idea. I mean, the Earth is messed up, but it would be a lot easier to terraform than Mars."

"That's what I've been trying to tell my co-workers here," Woody raised his hands, palms up.

"You can't fault people, latching onto a little hope," Leia said in their defense, even though she agreed with him.

"I just think they're looking for hope in all the wrong places," Woody said, then held out his plastic bag. It was full of muffins.

"Apple Walnut Muffin?"

Leia took one with a nod. It was much better than her oatmeal.

9:18 p.m.
95 Degrees Fahrenheit

That night, Leia got down on her knees and hugged her kids three or four times before putting on their breathing masks and turning out the light. Leia turned on the swamp cooler, but an hour later, it had already dropped down into the 60s outside.

Leia had never been more terrified in her life, but she didn't say a word about it to anyone. She didn't see the point of spreading the fear around.

10:22 a.m.
32 Degrees Fahrenheit

Leia sat in the break room and poked her oatmeal with a spoon, wanting to want to eat it, and failing.

"Cranberry Pecan Muffin?" Woody said, setting his bag of muffins on the table and acknowledging Leia with a jerk of his head.

Woody's muffins were much more appealing than her instant oatmeal.

"Hey, Tilly," Woody said, settling into his chair," They're hiring over at Orange Julius."

"Are you trying to get rid of me?" Tilly asked.

"Shit, no," Woody answered, just a little indignant," I already work there. That's how I know they're hiring."

Tilly leaned in. "In that case, thanks, I appreciate it, but I'm trying to go back to school and finish my nursing degree."

Leia missed Woody's reply because, at that moment, a small spark of pain shot from her second right bottom molar to her jaw. It was just a spark, though, and went away as soon as she switched to chewing on the other side.

9:42 a.m.
104 Degrees Fahrenheit

Leia was working pretty much exclusively at the launch site now.

She sat in her fresh-from-the-shop car halfway down the dusty road. She was a few minutes early so she pulled to the side of the road to watch the pallets of supplies and supply trucks on their way to the spaceship, like line after line of ants returning to the queen. The dashboard thermometer read one hundred and eight, three degrees higher than the display on her wrist. She wondered idly whether her watch or her car was right.

1:42 a.m.

99 Degrees Fahrenheit

That night, at Han's, Leia ground her back teeth so hard she broke the tooth that had been compromised by Woody's muffin. It happened in her sleep, but the fissure of pain split her tooth like lightning and woke her as sure as the sound of a gunshot. She could only think how it was her own fault for falling asleep after sex and being too vain to bring her night guard over to Han's. Too bad she hadn't met her dental deductible, and she was a month away from the end of the project. Money was about to become very tight very soon.

As she found her underwear and her socks, then the front door, the pain spread from her tooth to her jaw.

On the way home to shower, she stopped at the pharmacy, bought clove oil, and applied it directly to the tooth, mixed with the strongest pain reliever she could find. At work, she made a point not to stand too close to anyone.

By the time she headed home, the ache rolled like a continuous stream of thunder through every part of her above the collar, pulsing louder and louder by the moment.

The first thing she did when she got home was go to the garage and get a pair of pliers. Then she took a hot pan holder from the counter. Leia held the pliers in the flame. That would kill any bacteria, right?

Beside her, in the long narrow kitchen, Jasmine was poking a round ball of yeast with one finger.

"What you doin', Lay?" Jasmine said.

"I'm gonna need you to pull my toof," Leia mumbled, barely able to move her mouth for the pain.

Jasmine laughed, "You're kidding, right?"

"I bwoke my toof last night," Leia said.

"How? Didn't you have your guard in? Why didn't you have your guard in?" Jasmine's laughter turned to horror.

That was the million-dollar question, wasn't it?

"I fwogot it, duh," Leia let out, and it wasn't a lie.

"Well, go to the damn dentist," Jasmine said, and Leia knew she was right. "Use a damn credit card. Now is not the time to be cheap."

"The pwoject's ending soon, and I won't be able affowd anodder bill," Leia said because she knew it was the truth.

"No way..." Jasmine said, shaking her head. "I don't even think I could physically do it if I wanted to."

"Tilly! Budda-Cup!" Leia called, and the two came running.

"She wants you to pull her tooth so she doesn't have to pay for a dentist," Jasmine informed them and made it sound like an accusation in the process.

"No, and I am saying this because I love you," Tilly said.

"Are you nuts? I didn't go to dental school," Buttercup said, turning to Jasmine and Tilly. "Did you go to dental school?"

Leia took a deep breath to keep from either throwing up or passing out from the pain, and wrapped the pliers in a clean dish towel.

"Where are you going?" Tilly asked.

"To find someone who doesn't love me too much to help me out," Leia said, although she doubted it made sense to anyone but her. "I'll be back in time to put the kids to bed."

The thermometer read forty-two degrees, and Leia headed straight for Han's place.

The thermometer read eighty-seven and the clock read 7:01 p.m. when she got to 4444 Brilliant Way.

"You're serious? You want me to pull your tooth?" Han said when she finally explained what she wanted.

"If you want to be more than fuck buddies, here's your chance," Leia said, holding out the pliers. "Wait. Wash your hands first."

Fifteen minutes later, Leia was sitting on a chair on Han's back porch, and Han was standing with the pliers in Leia's mouth.

"You're sure you want me to do this? You can still change your mind," Han said.

"Aggggaahhhh!" Leia said, shaking her head remembering at the last minute not to scream. Han's kids were there and so was his mysterious unseen brother. She'd rather not have to interact with any of them. Still it was hard to modulate her volume because all she could hear was the roar of blood in her head. Somehow, the pain refused to stay in the approximate one square inch of molar where it belonged. Instead, it insisted on radiating down her jaw and down to the shoulder on the corresponding side. It leached out to the ends of her hair and spread until her spine ached and all the skin on her body pulsed with pain. The sooner that fucking tooth was gone, the better.

"Yes, I'm sure," Leia enunciated, taking care not to lisp but not entirely succeeding.

"I'm ready if you are," Han said unevenly, but it sounded like he wanted her to change her mind.

"I need this toof out of my mouf," Leia mumbled, too hurting and tired to make the words clear.

"Promise you won't blame me if anything goes wrong?" Han pleaded.

Leia slumped in frustration. They had been over this repeatedly.

"NO, I WILL NOT HOLD YOU WESPONSIBLE JUST PULL MY FUCKING TOOF ALWEADY," Leia whisper-shouted as quietly as she could.

Leia watched Han brace himself and stifled the urge to roll her eyes. Instead, she reached into her hip pocket and pulled out a plastic pint bottle of midgrade vodka.

"'Scuse me," she muttered, unscrewing the cap, seeing Han's look of judgment and hesitation and chalking it down as duly noted.

"Purely medicinal," she excused herself and proceeded to down the entire pint in three struggling swallows.

It felt like fire, and she sputtered and coughed for longer than she expected.

"You okay?" Han was always solicitous, whether she appreciated it or not.

When the painful spasms in her throat died down, Leia wiped her eyes and settled back on the kitchen chair.

"Let's get this over with,"

...And opened her mouth wide.

Han loomed over her. The pliers were cold in her mouth. Leia didn't expect the heat from the stove to have dissipated so completely. Han seemed to be having trouble positioning the pliers or getting a grip and then... and then... he took a deep breath and, without warning, pulled with all his might.

The pain was searing, like lightning electrifying her entire body. Leia was instantly consumed by regret. Han wasn't pulling her bad tooth, Han was breaking her jaw. She had been so bent on not spending a dime, and now she was going to bankrupt herself with a broken bone she couldn't conceivably ignore or treat at home. How much did a broken jaw cost? How was she going to take care of her kids if she couldn't work? There was a sharp crack, and pain was all she could think of, all she knew, and then... it wasn't.

Almost instantaneously, she was aware of two things. The first was that the pain was gone. The second was that a mouthful of blood was threatening to choke her.

Leia shoved Han out of the way on her race to the bathroom sink. But once she got there, the blood was followed down the sink by vodka and a considerable portion of bitter yellow bile.

Han reproached her immediately, "You haven't been eating."

"It hurt too much," she told him, then spat in the sink one last time.

The thermometer read ninety-nine.

There was one thing Leia hadn't foreseen, besides relief. It was impossible to go through certain things with another person without growing closer one way or another. Still, as soon as she'd staunched the flow of blood, she drove herself home.

7:42 p.m.
99 Degrees Fahrenheit

"Mamamamamamamama," Castor and Pollux met her at the door. "Where did you go? You missed supper."

"I went to get some help from a friend. My tooth was hurting me," Leia said.

"What friend?" Castor asked.

"You got a friend that's a dentist?" Pollux asked.

"Who do you know that we don't know? Is it from work?" Castor said.

"A space...dentist?" Pollux said.

"Not exactly," Leia said.

"Was it Aunty O?" Caster asked. "Did Aunty O pull your tooth?"

"Wanna see where they pulled it out?" Leia pulled back her lip, and they were both immediately distracted.

"Pick me up! I wanna see, too," Flower hollered as she ran towards them, her little flat feet slapping on the vinyl kitchen floor.

Buttercup stood at the sink, washing the dishes, not even looking in Leia's direction, shaking her head. The thermometer beside her on the wall read eighty-six.

2:43 a.m.
89 Degrees Fahrenheit

Four days later, Leia stood in the doorway to Han's kids' room with a finger to her lips. Han's two girls, Elizabeth and Tuni, who he called Pahtsi and Nami, were sleeping in their bed. Pahtsi was snoring. Nami was drooling. In the crib, Han Jr. was standing up, babbling. His mask lay twisted on the crib mattress. Apparently, he was big enough to take it off himself.

"ssshhhhhhhhhhhh," Leia whispered from the darkened doorway.

"Dadadadadadadaadadada," Han Jr. shouted with joy, waving at her with both arms.

Leia wasn't up to being introduced to all Han's kids at that moment or hiding out in his room until the coast was clear, so she made an executive decision and crept in to sweep Jr up in her arms. Not sure what else to do, she snuck away carefully while Jr laughed and babbled. The back porch seemed like a good place to get him quieted down. She sat down on the step and adjusted Jr. in her arms. There was a five degree difference between her watch and the old alcohol thermometer nailed beside the back door.

"I don't know if it's going to be okay or not, but I do know getting all worked up about it isn't going to help anything," she said as Jr. petted her face.

She started to rock him gently from side to side as he quieted down, not sure who was comforting who. She was always mesmerized by the moon. If she could sing without sounding like a sick cat, she would have sung him a song. A song for Jr. and the Moon.

Something was starting to happen in the back of Leia's head, and she felt it coming like a wave, getting progressively harder to ignore.

4:07 a.m.
89 Degrees Fahrenheit

When Leia got home an hour or so later, she got down on her knees in the children's dark room. Her own kids; Flower, Castor, and Pollux, her nieces and nephew; Alex and Andy, and Emmet, all asleep in their bunks. Daisy in her crib by the door. Their breathing machines humming softly.

Leia had no idea why tears were streaming down her face. The indoor thermometer read sixty-six and holding.

She struggled to keep her sobs silent as all the knowledge she'd held tucked away in the back of her mind struck her hard in the middle of her chest. A few hours later, she went to work just the same.

The thermometer in her office read thirty-two when Leia sat down to fill out forms. It read seventy-four when she headed home. They were having supper at Olga's that night.

7:03 p.m.
101 Degrees Fahrenheit

Leia was so tense and had held herself so stiff for so long that by the time she and her sisters, and her kids and her sisters' kids, not to mention Tilly and Daisy, tumbled out of the van and into the deep ruts that served as the driveway in front of Olga's trailer, every single muscle in her body hurt.

Her eyes hurt from crying. Every move she made felt like a burden. What she wanted to say, what she wanted to do, felt like a heavy rock lodged at the base of her throat, unwilling to move. A stone made of money and power and law. Law, based not on right or wrong but on the idea that might makes right. Law written without bothering to consult people like her and hers. All Leia had on her side was the inability to accept what she knew was coming. The inability to continue to sit still while everyone she knew and loved got screwed over one more time.

From Leia's point of view, everything seemed to be taking place in slow motion.

Olga opened the door, and she was as warm and sweet-smelling as ever. Persephone raced around to find Flower and hoist her up on her back.

They didn't deserve what was coming. None of them did. If every single working person on Earth had recycled their water three times before flushing it and swore off plastics forever, it wouldn't be a drop in the bucket of the waste and pollution coming from the wealthiest forty families on the planet.

Not coincidentally, these were the exact same families who had all the first class tickets to Mars on the three ships Leia had been working on since the twins were born.

It was happening because Leia, like everyone else, was sitting there letting it happen. Leia knew she had been complicit for a long time, but she didn't know if she had it in her to be complicit much longer. But it was one thing to understand what was going on and it was something else entirely to stick your neck out and do something about it. With the launch now just weeks away, Leia realized she had very little to lose. Still, it was terrifying.

Olga was a great cook, aside from being a complete wuss about chiles. Unfortunately, every bite Leia took tasted like ashes. She found herself standing up in the middle of the meal.

"I... I want to tell you something," Leia said, her voice still sounding caught in her throat.

"What?" Tilly asked. "Is this about your boyfriend?"

Leia cleared her throat again and took a sip of water. "No, this is important."

She wasn't looking for a laugh, but she got one. It caught hold of Jasmine first but ripped through all of them eventually, all of them except Leia. She meant it. Men, no matter how good-looking, didn't matter much compared to actual survival.

"No, I mean it," Leia said. "You know about the Mars mission.

You know they're not coming back for us. They don't give a shit what happens to us."

"Tell us something we didn't know, Lay-Lay," Olga snorted, still laughing.

"They are rich white people, aren't they?" Jasmine said.

"What's your point, Leia?" Buttercup said.

"Yeah, where are you going with this, Cuz?" Tilly asked.

"Ship number 2, the Futura, is stocked and ready now. I say we take it. I've been thinking about it, and I believe I know exactly how to do it," Leia said in a rush now that the thought had broken free and turned into speech.

"So how... exactly?" Buttercup asked. "What are you going to do? Hit the guards over the head with a club? Lure them away with a sandwich on a string?"

"I'm going to get past the guards by inviting them to come with us and bring their families with them," Leia said. "It's Memorial Day weekend. We call up all our folks in Oklahoma. If they get stopped on the road, they can tell the cops they're going to the big pow-wow up at Isleta."

Tilly was biting her lip, rocking slightly in her seat. "It might work. Those guards make $9.25 an hour."

"How do you know?" Buttercup asked.

"I know 'cause I have that job. I am a guard, remember?" Tilly said.

"You mean it, don't you? How is that even possible? Have you lost your freaking mind? Even if you do get away with it, how are you gonna turn a bunch of nurses and pow-wow singers into astronauts?" Buttercup said, her drawn-on eyebrows getting closer and closer and her lips getting thinner and thinner.

"Can you do it?" Jasmine asked, less of an accusation and more of a genuine question. "Is it possible? Can you take us to Mars?"

"We can do it," Olga said with a quiet assurance that was more convincing than all Leia's hot-headed sarcasm combined.

"It's like cars," Leia tried to explain.

"Like cars, how?" Buttercup asked, less skeptical now that Olga was clearly on Leia's side, but still cautious.

Olga had half a roll in her fist as she answered, "When the first cars came on the market, it took three people to start them. Nowadays, you don't even have to drive it yourself, provided you can afford the high-end option. It's how technology works. It tends to get simpler to operate over time."

"But a spaceship..." Buttercup protested.

"Apollo 11 had a massive ground crew plus 30 engineers in the control room," Leia explained. "But the Futura needs, I mean really needs, two live button-pushers in the control room. The Guided Launch System handles everything else."

"That's how progress works, making things simpler on the user end," Olga agreed.

"Which means you still have to find two people willing to stay behind," Buttercup pointed out.

"I have some candidates," Leia said.

"The first thing we need to do is get together everybody we'd take with us if we were never going to see this planet again," Jasmine said.

"And have them meet us Saturday at the launch site," Leia said.

"There's no way Chuy could make it, even if I could talk him into going AWOL," Buttercup said.

"Try, okay? You two haven't been together more than six months the entire time you've been married. This is your chance," Leia said, keeping to herself the thought that more time than that together might mean the end of their marriage.

Jasmine and Tilly pulled their phones out of their purses and started dialing. Leia hoped she didn't wind up stuck in space with too many people she couldn't stand.

"That's pretty short notice Lay-lay. Are you sure it's reasonable?" Olga said.

"Of course it's not reasonable, but it's the only way to do it. The longer we wait, the more likely it is someone else is going to be able to figure out what we're trying to do and stop us. If we're going to go, we need to do it within the next three days," Leia said.

Buttercup turned to Leia with her hand over the receiver. The thermometer read 99.

"How many do we have room for?" Buttercup asked.

"The ship is outfitted and supplied to hold four hundred but we need two hundred and fifty people minimum for a viable population," Leia said. "But we're not going to Mars. We're going to make the Futura into a generational ship."

"What's that?" Buttercup asked, and Buttercup hated asking Leia anything.

"It means a ship our descendants will live on for the foreseeable future," Olga said. "and we can manage it if we're diligent about maintenance."

"Is it a good idea, though?" Jasmine asked.

"It's a better idea than going to Mars," Olga said.

"Or staying here," Leia added.

Leia drew a map of the backroads of New Mexico in her food with a fork. A cooking thermometer lodged in the mashed potatoes read one hundred forty-six.

"Okay, tell them to take highway 285 and pack like they're going to a pow-wow. They'll be a lot of police out. Tell them what to say if they get stopped. And tell our mother if she starts any of her back-biting bullshit, I'm shoving her out the nearest airlock for the common good," Leia said, wondering if they realized she was utterly and completely serious.

10:38 p.m.
42 Degrees Fahrenheit

Leia caught Chaz on the sidewalk in front of her house.

"Hey, Princess Leia," Chaz muttered under his breath, eyes trained on the ground in front of him. "You wouldn't have five dollars, would ya ?"

"If you can follow some simple instructions, I'll give you a lot more than that," Leia said, keeping her voice low.

"Is it legal?" Chaz asked, raising his head.

"No," Leia admitted. "But I can keep you from being identified."

"How much?" Chaz asked, lowering his head again.

"Eight thousand," Leia was careful not to say it too loudly.

Chaz seemed frightened by the idea and shook his head vigorously without looking up. "That's too much. How about five hundred?"

This was not how Leia had imagined it going. "Ummm, okay," she said. "It's a deal. Meet me at my place Sunday morning, bright and early, but you're going to have to come in the back way."

"That's cool. I can climb the fence," Chaz said, brightening.

As he sauntered away happily, it occurred to Leia that while Chaz might be her ally, she was not necessarily his.

7:35 a.m.

31 Degrees Fahrenheit

Leia was not, generally speaking, much of a mall person, but under current circumstances, she made an exception. She searched out the most generic clothes in her wardrobe. She put on a black N95 that covered her face up to her eyes and she wore her glasses. Even though her car was out of the shop, she took the bus. The only purchase she made was at Orange Julius. The next step would be harder.

10:00 p.m.
80 Degrees Fahrenheit

In the shadow of the Futura, Sarah's response was immediate. She didn't even pause to consider.

"I just have one question: can you fly it?"

"Not only can we fly it, if anything goes wrong, between the two of us, Olga and I are as likely as anybody to be able to fix it," Leia said.

"You called it, Jerome," Sarah said into her headset.

"Where is Jerome tonight anyway? I thought he was on duty. I want to make sure he comes," Leia said.

"Sure enough, he's got closed circuit duty 'til... 2:00 a.m.," Sarah said.

"He says you're going to have to wait two days so he can get his folks down from Kotzebue. That okay?" Sarah asked.

"My sister and Olga wanted more time anyway," Leia replied with a shrug.

Those next two days ran from 102 Fahrenheit to 31 Fahrenheit and were hard on her nerves, but Leia made it through.

———

7:32 p.m.
98 Degrees Fahrenheit

Across Oklahoma, Comanches got in their cars. They were in brand-new red trucks. They were in sedans with mufflers dragging. They brought their family photo albums. They brought their regalia. They brought their oldest and most cherished hand-me-downs and heirlooms. A few came in rented or borrowed vehicles, but they came.

———

4:12 a.m.
56 Degrees Fahrenheit

Their last morning on Earth started with a loud bang and rattle of glass at the back door. Leia wandered in first, still asleep enough to be confused. Tilly and Jasmine were right behind her, rubbing their eyes. Leia peered closer at the glass only to recognize Chaz grinning and waving on the other side of the door.

Leia opened the door.

Chaz looked from one woman to the other. "You said be here bright and early."

"Bright being the operative term," Leia pointed out. "Meaning when the sun is up."

"Never mind, come in," Jasmine ordered him.

7:23 a.m.

62 Degrees Fahrenheit

"This seems wrong," Chaz was showered, in a clean security uniform, and his face covered in a thick layer of brown foundation, Fenty-490 Deep Cool to be exact. Leia hoped it was the foundation he was talking about as she stopped the car in front of the almost empty ground control offices.

"I know it does, but this is the only way past the cameras," Leia said, getting out of the car. "I'm the only one they'll see." To make sure of that, her face was covered with foundation, too, Fenty-110 Light Cool, the whitest make-up they made. "With any luck, I'll be long gone."

"How are you gonna get out?" Chaz asked, following her down the sidewalk.

"The camera only controls the way in. There's no monitor on the exit." Leia explained at the door.

Sarah smiled as she waved them in, although she blinked a few times at their reversed skin colors.

Woody was there beside her, but he didn't seem to notice their make-up.

As soon as they got to the lobby, Leia turned to look Chaz in the face.

"You stay right here. We'll be back in two, three minutes tops. Don't touch anything!" she said, grabbing hold of Woody's shirt and dragging him towards the women's bathroom.

As soon as the restroom door banged shut behind her, she stuck her hands in her jacket pockets and started pulling out stacks of cash.

"Here's everything I've got," Leia said. "You can have my car, too, but it's a piece of shit... and you've got to give Chaz five hundred bucks."

"Is that all?" Woody asked, two wrinkles in the bridge of his nose.

"I was going to split the money down the middle, but he says that's all he can handle. C'mon, let's get back before he breaks something or gets scared and runs." Leia opened the women's room door.

8:02 a.m.
94 Degrees Fahrenheit

Olga paced around the cockpit, readying everything she could think of.

8:04 a.m.
92 Degrees Fahrenheit

To anyone else, it might seem irrational, but her current task was the most nerve-wracking part of the entire plan as far as Leia was concerned. In fact, she didn't mention it to Buttercup because she knew her sister would make fun of her for it. With more care than she'd taken with anything in her life, Leia gently, oh so gently, placed her stickers, numbered one through fifty-two, on the appropriate buttons. First, she did Woody's, then she did Chaz's. The problem wasn't the launch sequence, she had memorized that her first day in the control room. She could probably sing it in her sleep. Hell, she probably did sing it in her sleep. The problem was Leia had always been heavy-handed and awkward, and she was terrified of accidentally pressing a button while applying her numbered stickers.

"They're coming off. I mean, they aren't on all the way, your little stickers," Chaz said, watching her with microscopic care.

"But you see where they are? What button they're on? You can read the numbers, right?"

"Well, yeah," Chaz admitted.

"That's gonna have to be good enough," Leia said, cold anxiety pulsing through her body.

"Don't worry, I got it," Woody said.

"Thank you," Leia said, sure she'd never meant anything so much in her life.

There was a knock at the control room door, loud enough that Leia, Woody, and Chaz jumped to attention and then relaxed, just as reflexively when they heard Sarah's voice.

"Are you ready? Your sisters said to tell you they're waiting on us," Sarah said through the door.

"On my way," Leia turned to Woody and Chaz. "I'll let you know when count down starts. Don't start until I give you the word."

8:16 a.m.
96 Degrees Fahrenheit

Outside, the Futura Buttercup helped the last of the family and their belongings board the ship. Inside, Jasmine made sure their friends, relatives, and random but necessary acquaintances stowed their belongings in the luggage-hold and then took their places in the launch s eats.

"Please keep your tray in the upright position until we achieve lift-off," Jasmine said, a wry smile twisting the corner of her mouth as the line of relatives seemed to slow and bunch up into a knot for a moment. "It's alright, Auntie. Leia isn't even here yet. You can take your time."

Their Aunt Kay gave her a warm hug. "You're my favorite stewardess."

⚓ 〰 ⚓

8:20 a.m.
98 Degrees Fahrenheit

Sarah's belly barely cleared the steering wheel of her Honda Accord.

"So... uh... mind if I ask you when you're due?" Leia felt both intrusive for asking and embarrassed that she didn't already know.

"The 18th, but my other two were both two weeks late," Sarah said matter-of-factly.

It was the twentieth. But it wasn't as if there was any way to avoid having babies on the ship in the long run. Putting it off would not make it any easier. Might as well rip off the reproductive band-aid and have a baby right away.

All mine were late," Leia agreed, trying not to think about all the things that could go wrong with either the launch or the birth.

Neither of them was able to think of much else to say until they arrived at the launch site. There were cars everywhere. Leia recognized most of them. It looked like everyone but Buttercup and the kids had boarded.

Leia unlocked her car door, beginning to breathe a sigh of relief.

It should have been a given that this was the moment where something went wrong.

A car peeled into the site, already dusty from a thousand trips down the strip of dirt road. Oh shit, it was Whitman, red-faced and angry.

Leia struggled with her seat belt. She had no idea what Whitman was saying, but he was out of his car now, and Buttercup was advancing on him. Buttercup's expression was flat, her hands were raised palm outward, her purse slung over her shoulder.

"Where's the buckle on this thing?" she asked Sarah, desperate to stop Whitman before he stopped the Futura.

"There isn't one, it's automatic. All you have to do is open the door," Sarah reminded her.

When Leia opened the door, Whitman turned to glare at her.

"What the fuck is this shit?" Whitman screamed, focusing all his white-hot rage in Leia's direction.

Buttercup took this as her opportunity, taking Whitman by one hand, bending and twisting his wrist at an angle human joints weren't evolved to bend at. He forgot all about Leia. His knees buckled, and he pitched forward. Buttercup changed the angle of his wrist a degree or two, and Whitman fell flat on his face in the dirt. Buttercup knelt, one knee wedged securely between Whitman's shoulder blades.

Whitman continued to splutter incoherently. It sounded like, "Dude, dude, dude, What the fuck? What the fuck? What the actual fuck?"

"Open my purse, will you?" Buttercup asked as Leia approached. The children, holding hands, watched from what they must have figured was a safe distance.

"What am I looking for?" Leia asked, pulling back the zipper.

"Zip ties and hypodermic needles," Buttercup said brusquely.

"Do you always have this shit in your purse?" Leia asked, openly incredulous.

"Sure, you never know when you're gonna need to hog-tie some-body." Buttercup was breathing hard. "Of course not, it was just in case we ran into any trouble."

"And we did," Leia said.

"Zip tie?" Buttercup held out her free hand.

Leia watched as her boss's hands were secured.

"Shot?" Buttercup extended her hand once more.

"What's in it?" Leia asked, handing it over.

"Thorazine. On the unit, we don't usually keep a patient restrained once they've been sedated."

"You know best. If you think he's safe to let go..."

Buttercup squinted for a long second and, reaching into Whit-man's back pocket, took his cell phone and, reaching back like a pro-fessional pitcher, hurled Whitman's phone with all her might. The phone sailed through the air in an elegant arc before skipping along the sagebrush raising clouds of dust and rocks as it went.

"Just goes to show, huh?" Leia said, wishing she had pockets to put her hands in.

"Goes to show what?" Buttercup asked, tilting her head a few degrees.

"In the heart of the most mild-mannered Comanche is a horse thief just waiting for the chance to come out." Leia was suddenly filled with a strange sense of optimism.

"We can say that once we get into space," Buttercup reminded her.

No doubt Leia would have made time to argue with her sister if her children hadn't come rushing up.

"Come on, I got room for all three of you," Leia said, wrapping her arms around all three at once, the twins on either side, Flower Array in the middle.

"What's happening?" Pollux asked. "What are we doing, exactly? Are we stealing this ship?

"We're going to space, baby, and we have as much right to the ship as anyone else. More maybe, and we're taking everybody we love with us," Leia said sniffing his head and thinking back to when he and Castor were her tiny babies.

"All of us, everybody?" Flower asked, gesturing to the line of cars and trucks, mostly older models, dusty from the dirt roads, a single file line on the pothole-marked dirt road leading to the launch site.

"Yeah, all of us, baby. You and me and your bubbas. Everybody from our house. All our friends and relatives that wanted to come," Leia snuggled them close, knowing before long she was going to have to leave them to Jasmine and Tilly and make her way to the cockpit.

"Even the space-dentist?" Castor asked.

Leia hesitated before she answered that one. Han wasn't exactly a space-dentist by any stretch of the imagination, but that was who Castor was referring to, and he and his kids were already there. She'd made sure.

"Yeah, he's around here, some place," Leia said as her eyes searched for his vehicle. Against her will her glance went back repeatedly to Whitman on his hands and knees, looking for his phone, dopily, in slow motion.

In the cockpit Leia and Olga looked over the controls, trying to pretend they weren't covered with goosebumps, everything that possibly could go wrong racing through their heads.

"I don't know what we would have done if Sarah and Jerome hadn't talked the other security guards into cooperating," Olga said, doing the fourth systems check of the morning.

"I dunno, stayed here with the rest of the planet." Leia shrugged. "I don't know what we would have done if they weren't handling the boarding."

"We haven't made lift-off yet." Olga was calm, clear-eyed, and sharp. Leia knew they were both doing the same act.

"But we will," Leia said, because she knew it without question.

"You're being very optimistic... for you," Olga put it very nonchalantly, but the accusation was clear.

"And you're being very pessimistic... for you," Leia handed it right back to her.

You're scared. I'm scared, but what else can we do?

"Eh, not so much pessimistic as unsure," Olga admitted.

Leia shrugged. "Sometimes you just know what's going to work and what isn't. Like when I married what's-his-face. I stood there in the judge's chambers and I knew it was a mistake. This is just like that only in reverse. I know it's going to happen and I know it's going to go off without a hitch."

Olga burst out laughing. "Lay-Lay, that has got to be the single most positive thing you have said in the entire time I've known you and yet you managed to say it in the most negative way imaginable."

"What can I say? I'm predictable," Leia smiled as she said it.

"I wouldn't say predictable so much as oh... I don't know... cartoonish, maybe," Olga said.

Leia put her hand to her chest in mock offense "Cartoonish? I'm wounded!"

"Yeah, yeah, yeah," Leia choked out, laughing and rolling her eyes, maybe she was just trying to appear nonchalant, maybe she was verging on hysteria." Ready to call Woody and commence countdown?"

"No reason to delay further. Let's get started," Olga said.

Leia checked her monitors and scrutinized what the cameras showed her; friends and relatives strapped to the walls of the lower decks, like in a carnival ride. Uncle Boy's eyes were wide and his smile so forced he looked like he was on the verge of tears. Her Aunt Viola was crying. Han's hands were knotted into fists. Everyone was looking nervous. Strike that; everyone was looking terrified. Two different babies cried loudly. Pahtsi and Nahmi opened their mouths and joined the babies. Flower looked at Persey out of the corner of her eye for reassurance. The thermometer read seventy and as long as the ship was functioning properly it would stay that way.

Leia leaned toward the intercom "Han? Could you do something to... entertain people, or something?"

Han, strapped to the wall, looked stunned "Uh sure I guess." and cleared his throat "Soobeesu," he practically yelled, and Leia reflexively moved back from the intercom.

"What's that mean?" someone, it sounded like one of a dozen different teenagers, asked.

"It means a long time ago," someone else explained.

"Back when we had no horses, only dogs, and there were no taibos," Han said.

"Is that a thing? I mean, was that a real time?" another teenager asked.

An older person snorted.

"Yes, it was real. Like I said, back when we only had dogs to pull our packs but after we split with the Shoshone," Han trudged on, bravely.

"Did we really used to be Shoshones?" asked the same teenager as before, who was either raised under a rock or deeply committed to giving Han a hard time.

"Duh, why do you think we have the Shoshone reunion?" someone else said.

"ANYWAY," Han shouted "In those days we used to go all over to trade, even though we were walking everywhere, and there was one band who went way down south and traded with the Nauhautl because our languages were related so we could make ourselves understood to each other. And when they got there the people they usually traded with had had a...like...a catastrophe..."

"What happened to 'em?"

"The Spanish came," Han said "And a lot of people said we should hightail it out of there before they do to us what they did to those folks we used to trade with."

"And did they?"

"There was one woman, not young and not old, and she had a track record of having good ideas, and she said if we had some of those Spanish horses we'd be set. She said what we ought to do was send a bunch of young men to get captured. And then in one year, when they had learned all about horses they could steal all the horses they could lay their hands on and rendezvous with the rest of their band, further n orth."

"And after talking it over that's just what they did, and they brought a bunch of the Nauhautl people they had been enslaved along side, with them," Han said.

Frankly, Leia had been expecting a longer story.

"That's not the way I heard it," someone said.

"Well, I heard your version of how we got horses, Clyde, and neither one of these stories is the way my Grandma told me," an unidentified woman told Clyde.

"Maybe different bands got horses different ways. Maybe we got the first horses a coupla different times," some rare reasonable soul said.

Any excuse to argue among themselves. Leia felt vaguely reassured, while Han hadn't turned out to be a storyteller for the ages at least he had provided them something to disagree about, and that was distraction enough.

Leia pressed the intercom button. "Now commencing countdown."

"Mission control?" Olga said, addressing the monitor.

"Hello, Olga, Hello Leia," Woody said "Everything ready over there?"

"Ready as we'll ever be, I think," Olga said.

"Hi, Leia," Chaz broke in "I wanted to let you know, because, you know, this is probably my last chance, if I had my shit together, I would have asked you out, you know. I think we would have been good t ogether."

Leia had no idea how to take that. It was... it was a weird thing to say and not a thing she really wanted to think about but, under the circumstances she didn't want to upset Chaz.

"Thank you, Thank you very much, Chaz," she said stiffly.

On the internal monitor Leia could see movement. She zoomed in closer. A man in a Ramones t-shirt was unbuckling himself. It looked like her cousin, Kelly. It was her cousin Kelly.

Leia pressed the intercom again. "What are you doing, Kelly?"

"I know what we can do to help everybody chill out," Kelly said, racing out of the launch seat.

"Whatever you're going to do, do it fast, will you!" Leia shouted over the 'com. "We're about to start the countdown!"

She watched, pissed off as on a different monitor Kelly raced down the ladder to the storage compartment. Plaid shirt flying.

"Without a hitch, huh?" Olga asked.

Leia didn't answer, there was no point. The roar of the engines made it impossible to hear anything. Instead she gave Olga an irritated glance as Kelly buckled himself back to the wall, now holding a hand drum and drum stick.

Leia watched on the monitor as Woody and brown-faced Chaz began prepping the sequence.

"We start with one, right?" Chaz asked Woody.

"No, we start at fifty-two and end at one," Woody said, reaching over to mash Chaz's first button for him.

"Oh, yeah, I remember now," Chaz said defensively.

Leia watched her read-outs.

Olga leaned over and without a word squeezed Leia's hand for the briefest instant.

Leia, too, remained quiet but inside she whispered a prayer of thanks. More than any other adult in her life Olga was precious to her. Even when they occasionally stumbled or let each other down she was precious.

Woody's voice rang out across the cockpit and Leia pushed down the intercom switch so the entire ship could hear.

"Ten,"

"Nine,"

"Eight,"

"Seven,"

"Six,"

"Five,"

"Four,"

"Three,"

"Two,"

"We'll be seeing you,"

On the internal monitor Kelly's face and the faces around him distorted from the force of the lift-off.

Despite the force, Kelly and fully half the people she could see on the monitor were singing.

Leia's bones rattled and she wished she'd thought to put her mouth guard in. It was hard not to grind her teeth as she kept a close eye on all the ship's systems.

"Only three more minutes until we leave the atmosphere," Leia said.

"Aye-Aye, Captain," Olga saluted, her eyes sparkling.

"I am not the captain, uh uh, don't even play like that..."

"Those mother fuckers," Olga cursed quietly and Leia's blood ran cold. Olga never swore. Not even King could make her swear.

On the radar screen two objects raced toward them. Nuclear Missiles. Nukes were coming at them. The path looked wonky but it didn't need to be a direct hit. She couldn't change the Futura's trajectory until they left the atmosphere. Either they were going to get hit or they weren't. Either they were going to live or they were going to die.

"I guess they know we're gone," Leia said, forcing the hot blood to run cold again in her veins "I hope Chaz and Woody get out okay."

This was what Leia got for saying the ship was going to get off without a hitch. They were all going to die and it was going to be her fault.

No.

It was not a rational thought and Leia didn't have that kind of power. Leia looked at the radar and quickly calculated the trajectory of both the Futura and the missiles.

"They're too late," Olga pointed out. "I don't think they're going to hit us. They can't. We'll be out of the atmosphere before they reach our position. The best they can hope for is to hit our boosters after we separate."

"There are too many failsafes, they couldn't launch in time to hit us," Leia sighed with bone deep relief the second she realized it was true.

"They're still mother fuckers, though," Olga said.

"Am I arguing with you?" Leia said.

On the interior monitor Leia could see the people, still strapped in, mouths open, all being pulled in one direction. There was Kelly with his drum near the center of the screen. Fear and fatigue were clearly starting to infect people. Every single child's face was greased with tears and mucus. She wished she had another self, three other selves, to go down and comfort each of her kids separately. Even if it were possible it wouldn't matter, because those selves would be strapped to the wall, too, for safety's sake. And if they weren't strapped down, the Gs would have them pinned to the floor.

Leia silently offered encouragement to Kelly and the other singers.

She could see Kelly kick at the person beside him, their cousin Mickey, mouthing something. If she had to guess she would imagine he said.

Keep singing. C'mon, Mickey.

And then they broke free.

Olga switched on the 'com.

"Lift-off is complete. We've left Earth's atmosphere. You may now move freely about the ship," Olga said.

Leia laughed. "Don't forget to tell them a stewardess will be around in a few minutes with those little bags of peanuts."

"Don't remind me, I am so hungry. There should be some food stashed away somewhere up here, shouldn't there?" Olga rifled through her seat and came up with a non-descript foil packet. "I knew it !"

"What you got?" Leia asked.

"Wasabi peas and goldfish and... some kind of power bar," Olga shook a bag of goldfish over her own head.

"A nutritional powerhouse if I ever saw one."

"Want some, Lay?" You can have the peas. I know they're your favorite."

"Absolutely," Leia said. "And I know you hate them."

PART II

Transition for Two Violas

F ifteen minutes later Leia was surprised to see Tilly at the door of the cockpit, baby Daisy on her hip. Behind her, like something from a cartoon, was the rest of her household, craning their necks to see Olga and her flying the ship.

"Hey," said a familiar voice but they would all be familiar voices from here on out.

Leia turned to see long lean Buttercup at the front of the gaggle with her kids.

A blink of an eye later those same two kids Alex and Andy, a boy and a girl and both made up mostly of knees and elbows, 10 and 11 years old respectively tumbled through the doorway, tripping one over the other.

"Yo, get your butts back here," big muscular Chuy, with his Army haircut and his eyes too close together, reached around Buttercup to pick the children he rarely saw up and pull them back out of the way.

"You got a license to fly this thing?" Jasmine asked her, all fake casual. Beside her small and silent as usual Emmet strained to see into the cockpit wedged between his cousins, Castor and Pollux.

Flower struggled to get out Jasmine's arms. Persey, of course, was in the mix standing on her tiptoes, spinning, moving like a human gyroscope. And then, somehow in the crowded doorway another face in the crowd, she saw Han struggling to insert himself near the door.

Shit.

"Leia, this is my brother, Sagan. Sagan, Leia Wurahapt... should be Wura Ohaptu... you know... Yellow Bear. Leia and I've kinda been seein' each other for a while," Han said, thrusting forward a short chubby guy in a band t-shirt and the same hair parted down the middle and in two skinny braids as half the Native men Leia knew. The guy didn't bear much resemblance to Han at all.

"What? How long?" Jasmine asked, her eyes bugging.

"Where, is what I want to know," Buttercup added, looking Han up and down.

Caught, Leia had no choice but to answer.

"Yeah, what he said... umm 'bout a year...his place pretty much exclusively. Han, these are my sisters Buttercup and Jasmine and Tilly and... the kids. Mine are Castor and Pollux, it'll take you a while to tell them apart and Flower's my little one. Buttercup's girls are Alex and Andy and Jasmine's boy is Emmet. Tilly's baby is Daisy," Leia explained, trying to get it all out as quickly as possible.

"You know Jr, and Betty and Thuni already," Han said but the truth was the only name Leia had been one hundred percent sure of was Jr's.

There was a period, in the very beginning, where Leia, and she was pretty sure Olga as well, lost track of time. Eventually, Leia was having tiny dreams every time she shut her eyes. Tricks of the light and both women's overworked eyes and brains rushed around the cockpit at regular intervals. There was more on both their plates than two people reasonably could do. First and foremost was teaching volunteers to perform routine ship's maintenance and piloting duties. Meanwhile someone else, or rather a whole slew of someone elses named Jasmine and Sarah and Leia's Aunt Kay, and Uncle Ben, got busy organizing everything that Olga and Leia weren't working on. Leia left everything not directly in front of her to whoever took it upon themselves to figure it out. Her plate was paper and couldn't hold any more.

Not living on a planet orbiting a star meant there was no observable day or night. Minutes ticked by and were recorded on the ship's computers but her body had no idea how long it was she worked. She showered when Olga told her she needed to. She napped in her seat when she couldn't stay awake. She ate when Jasmine came and prodded her to eat. And at a certain point she couldn't quite decide whether to count the time they had been gone in days or weeks. She left the cockpit, hoping someone had thought to assign her a cabin somewhere as she climbed down the ladder to the habitation level.

"Leia!" Buttercup called out "You're out of the cockpit."

"I hope somebody saved me a place to sleep. I need a bed, an actual human bed for sleeping, before I fall down," Leia said, fighting desire to groan, loudly.

"C'mon, like we'd forget about you," Buttercup said.

"I forgot about everything but the ship's systems for a while there," Leia said, shaking her head.

Buttercup rolled her eyes.

"Leia!" Han called, coming around the corner. "C'mon. Keem, I got somethin' I wanna show you."

Leia turned and looked at Buttercup.

"Go on, then. I guess Han's got something he wants to show you," Buttercup said, her expression sly." Although I figured you've already seen it by now. I mean you said you've been together a year already."

Han snorted, "Keem, all you Numunu waipun are so rugged."

Buttercup rolled her eyes and shook her head as if it was below her dignity to reply to accusations of ruggedness.

Leia personally thought if Comanche women were rugged it was because they had to be. She wondered if it was worth saying to Han.

"Keem," Han said again, pulling Leia along by her hand. She was too tired to think of a reason to resist.

He stopped in front of cabin 49 and the door slid open. The walls were painted night sky blue, and crimson red and deep golden yellow; Comanche flag colors. Leia's picture of her grandparents in their military uniforms was hanging over the bed. The bedspread was Han's prized wool blanket with a buffalo in the center. Leia couldn't help thinking it was too warm on the ship for a wool blanket.

Wait. Wait. Wait.

Her pictures on the wall. Han's blanket on the bed.

Shit.

While she was busy dealing with the things she knew no one else could do, her sisters were busy doing what they could do and what they could do was move her in with Han.

For a brief moment Leia considered raising a fuss. There was no way she had the energy to find herself her own room, let alone make it this comfortable. Last time she moved it had taken her a year to unpack completely.

What the hell, if her sisters and Han wanted to make Han her husband it was hardly worth her time to disagree. She was too tired to do anything but sleep.

On second thought, with just a sheet underneath, the wool buffalo blanket was kind of cozy. She barely noticed being watched as her eyes fell shut, hard and heavy.

Leia woke up to Olga sitting on the foot of her bed. Bouncing.

"You noticed that one, huh?" Olga said. "It's about time, Lay, You've only been asleep for a week."

Leia bolted upright ready to catapult herself out of bed and do whatever needed doing but Olga laughed again.

"Calm down, lay, I was just funnin' ya. More like fourteen... sixteen hours."

Leia let herself flop backwards onto her pillow, groaning. "I still need to get up."

"Yes, so you can eat something because I know your blood sugar is all over the place, and shower because you are also rather ripe." Olga wiggled her nose.

"Yeah." Leia sat up, but more slowly this time. "And as soon as I've done all that I'll get back to work."

"That's not strictly necessary," Olga said.

"What are you talking about?" Leia's heart started to pound as it dawned on her that the fact that Olga was sitting on her bed meant she was not in the control room "Who's flying this thing?"

"Malena," Olga said matter-of-factly.

"Do you know how many traffic tickets that girl has?" Leia was dumbfounded.

"Not really," Olga shrugged. "We cleared the moon thirteen hours into our flight, there isn't anything for her to hit out there right now."

"What if all I can think about are all the other things that could theoretically go wrong?" Leia tried her best to make her point.

"Aren't you always doing that?" Olga reminded her. "Look, there are no jobs and no bills out here. There are two hundred ninety-three adults on board this ship and the only thing that has to be done is routine maintenance and piloting the ship, and we don't have anything better to do than teach them how to do it. Aren't you tired of being irreplaceable?"

"When you put it that way..." Leia left the thought unfinished as she fell back on her pillow a second time.

Three shifts later, Sarah's baby was born. Buttercup and Carla, who also happened to be a nurse, delivered her. She seemed healthy but her color was off. Not yellow. Not pink. Not especially brown. More bluish than anything else. There were no doctors on board but there was a comprehensive medical library and eighteen nurses. In the end, the diagnosis was low-grade *methemoglobinemia*. She would grow up to be blue. They'd keep an eye on the condition to make sure it didn't become a problem. Sarah named her Hope.

By the time Leia ate and showered and started checking out how everything was going, it seemed like everything that needed settling had been more or less sorted out by some other competent adult. It was kind of wonderful, being able to trust other people to be capable and work toward the common good. She was also a little teeny tiny bit worried about not feeling special any more but then, really, when was the last time she actually felt special? College maybe? Then she wondered if she'd really felt special in college or if she'd just been told she was special enough to allow herself to act like an asshole.

From then on she worked regular shifts but none of them were long. She played with her kids, which frankly she hadn't done in a long time, maybe she'd never done it before, at least not without being distracted.

Leia got out of bed, bathed, and dressed. She put on make-up and coveralls, because she liked to wear make-up and frankly, there was not a clothing style in the universe that she'd found flattered her fat-bellied flat-butted shape, and was practical for working on a spaceship. Then she piloted the ship for a few hours. Once, her baby-cousin Amber came in for a shift and Leia went down to see what was happening in the rest of the ship.

She came down the ladder only to find Jasmine handing out the food bars she usually passed around for breakfast.

"Soup's on!" Jasmine sang out pulling a chocolate berry pecan bar out of the basket and handing it to Leia.

"Mmmm, soup, my favorite," Leia laughed, shoving half the bar in her mouth, preparing to ask if Jazz thought the kids would be out of class soon.

"Extra chunky, you might say." Jazz said, balancing the basket on her head.

Sagan came loping up, at the same time struggling with a pair of jeans that refused to fit quite right, dragging the ground and threatening to trip or humiliate him.

"Leia," Sagan huffed awkwardly, still winded. It was the closest Leia had seen him come to physically exerting himself. Han, on the other hand, jogged through the habitation levels every day.

"What's up?" Leia asked.

Sagan lowered his head and extended his clipboard, mumbling non-stop the entire time in that low breathy all-one-word way of his.

"IhadanideaIfwecanemptyoneofthehabitationlevelsanddivertthep lumbingwastethereinsteadofjettisoningitwecansterilizeitandconvertit

tofertilizerO...Olgasaidthewastegetsjettisonedbutifwefollowmyplanw
ithinayearwecanhavethestartofasustainablefoodgarden."

Leia blinked while Sagan waited expectantly.

There were two problems with that. First of all, loud music in her
earphones had been Leia's biggest vice—men aside—since she was a
kid. She knew perfectly well she didn't hear as well as she ought to. On
the other hand Sagan rarely spoke above a whisper and he mumbled
literally everything he said. She had no idea how he'd instructed anyone about anything.

Leia stopped. She forced herself not to get sarcastic, as she stepped
closer.

"I don't hear so well, could you try that again," she said.

"I had... an... idea... If we can empty one of the habitation levels
and divert the plumbing waste there instead of jettisoning it, we can
sterilize it and convert it to fertilizer. O... Olga said the waste gets
jettisoned. Within a year, we can have the start of a sustainable food
garden." Sagan talked faster than any person Leia had ever met, still
holding out the clip board, presumably with details of the plan.

Leia bent over a clip board, flipping through the pages, there were
fifty-two of them.

"No shit?" Leia asked.

"Or, alternately, a whole lot of shit," Jasmine said.

"But... You're serious?" Leia brushed off Jazz's joke.

"It's not as strange as it sounds. Han says there are seeds and
frozen embryos of a thousand different species on the storage levels.
There's a lotofevidence the whole Amazonrainforest originated as a
humanengineered foodforestwithsuper super superenrichedsoil made
from charcoal and human waste. There's no logical reason we couldn't
create a paradise right here. We needtobeaclosedsystemifwe'regoing-
tobeself-sustaining..." mumbling though he was Sagan showed signs

of building up steam. Soon it would be impossible to get a word, much less a whole thought into his tangled mumbled talk.

Leia raised one palm in self-defense. "This looks good but it's going to take a little engineering on our part to figure out how to char the organic material and reroute the plumbing away from the airlock. Give me a little time to read through this and think about the logistics." Leia took the clipboard, preparing herself to have her mind blown by the possibilities. She was not disappointed.

Within what would have been a few months back on Earth, the whole population was putting into action Sagan's plan to turn the ship into a garden.

And then, one day, life was normal.

Their routine had become routine. The lack of bills and bosses and money. No stress to speak of, beyond the obvious hurtling through space in a tin can with no apparent destination, which wasn't so bad once you got used to it. And pretty much everyone was used to it now. People jockeyed for shifts doing maintenance or having pilot duty. The rest of the time they spent visiting with each other, tending to the kids, and above all they made things.

They made songs. Guys who never would have considered themselves singers tried to outdo each other with morning songs when their waking shift started.

They made jewelry. When the beads they brought with them ran out, beaders took apart any old pieces they didn't absolutely love. Then they used those beads to make pieces they did love. Then the beaders promptly gave the pieces that they loved away.

They made toys out of old clothes, dolls mostly. All the kids wanted dolls, so all the kids had dolls. Even boys who wouldn't have been caught dead playing with dolls on earth had a "guy" as they called them. And because the boys called them guys, the girls started doing it, too. All the dolls were guys now. It was a kid thing, near as Leia could figure.

They danced and sang every day, it seemed to Leia, even though there weren't really distinct "days" anymore, only alternating work, play, and sleep shifts. Still they had brought themselves with themselves so they were themselves. They carried the remnants of life on Earth in their speech. One day, though, and again Leia was well aware it was not a real day, Little Viola came to Leia.

"Hey!" Leia was genuinely happy to see Little Viola. She was her favorite of all the sullen teens on the ship. Leia got the whole sullen teen thing conceptually. She halfway felt she had only recently gotten out of the phase herself. So until puberty hit Flower like a runaway train, Little Viola was her favorite.

"We don't have any new clothes," Little Viola said, looking at something behind Leia's left shoulder.

Leia shrugged. She didn't have any power over that. While she was confident there was some way to make new clothes with the supplies they had on the ship, it was not anything that Leia had even noticed in the last year. She probably would not have noticed it for a very long time if Little Viola hadn't brought it up. She guessed they were going to need clothes sooner or later but until the day came when the only other option was nudity, Leia didn't really care. Leia was slightly pleased at the realization. There weren't many things she actively did not care about, at all.

"We just have the clothes we brought with us," Little Viola said in a monotone.

Leia started to shrug again and beg off when Little Viola continued, not exactly interrupting her elder.

"...The March Vogue 2030 has an article about growing cloth from different algae and umm... SCOBY and you know, kombucha?"

Leia didn't ask but she sure as hell didn't know what a SCOBY was.

"A SCOBY is the scum off the top of kombucha. And the computer says we got all that stuff in storage for uumm Mars," Little Viola, who was taller than Leia, said.

"We aren't going to Mars," Leia said automatically.

"I know that," Little Viola explained. It was obvious she was making an effort not to speak to Leia the way she would talk to another teenager. "But can I have them?"

Leia was confused. "Why are you asking me? I'm not in charge."

"Who am I supposed to ask then? Who is in charge?" Little Viola asked, clearly put out.

Leia looked around, hesitant to admit it might be up to her to grant anyone permission for anything. All in all, she felt fine saying no, but yes made her uncomfortable.

"Just don't use up all the Scooby," Leia said.

"It's called a SCOBY. Long o," Little Viola said.

"Or the algae, don't use it up or kill it all. Sagan gave me a lecture today about biodiversity," Leia felt a little nauseous from saying yes. She saw a little flicker, human shaped, on the right of her field of vision, knew it wasn't there, and rubbed her eyes to make it go away.

Little Viola looked at her like she was losing respect for her by the second. "I'm only going to need a little bit. It grows."

"That's good. Do it then. You have my permission," Leia tried not to sound awkward.

"And I'm gonna need a 3-D printer. One of the big ones," Little Viola added.

"What for?" Leia asked.

"To grow the cloth in. If I grow it in the right shape, I won't have to make any cuts, just sew." Little Viola went back to staring over Leia's shoulder.

"Umm okay," Leia said. "You can use one of the big printers."

"Thanks," Little Viola exhaled, which was when Leia realized Viola hadn't been angry, she'd been nervous. Worried Leia would say no.

Leia was coming to the conclusion that once the basics; food, water, oxygen, and functional plumbing were taken care of, humans tend to start getting in their own way again. They get stupid. At least if she was anything to go by.

There was no denying it, Leia's first inclination was to make bad choices.

Sagan, for instance, if she'd met him first Han wouldn't have had a chance. Yes, it defied all reason and common sense. That didn't make it any less true.

Han was an ideal man in every way she could think of. He woke up before her and got her coffee. Was attentive in bed. Took good care of the kids. Not just his kids and her kids but all the kids. He taught all the kids Numunu Tekwaru, and history, and math to the littles who didn't need to learn anything fancy yet. And he kept himself in shape. Good shape. Honestly Leia woke up every morning feeling like she'd won Han in a raffle.

And yet...

Every morning when Leia strapped on her tool belt and left their room, Han still picking clothes up off the floor, Leia looked forward to running into Sagan. He was nowhere near as handsome as Han. He didn't have a charming bone in his body. He tended to mumble, very quickly, in a monotone that was almost, but not quite, a whisper. He tried to keep his hair in a pair of skinny braids, but whole locks of hair were always escaping from their confines and sticking out at strange angles. The overalls he frequently wore, presumably to keep from sharing his ass-crack with everyone on the ship, didn't do his belly any favors.

And yet...

He was the most interesting person on the ship. He was full of interesting information on topics Leia didn't know jack about. He had a way of putting ideas together that was totally foreign to Leia. Sagan was weird and Sagan was fascinating.

Sagan was Han's brother.

Sagan was also a very bad idea.

There were less than three hundred people on the ship. Any break-ups were bound to cause problems, even if they were bound to happen eventually. It would be selfish and short-sighted for Leia to be the first. Besides, there was literally nothing wrong with Han. Nothing Leia could think of anyway. He treated her well. He treated her kids well. He had literally no bad habits she had noticed... yet.

Leia didn't want trouble so it was on her not to start any. Even though she longed to start trouble, she would hold herself in. Trouble and asteroids were the biggest existential threats they had right now.

So what if Han and Leia managed to wind up sharing a room without ever having a conversation about living arrangements. That was life sometimes. It wasn't about what you planned for, it was about what actually happened. It was probably for the best. Leia knew from experience her liking Sagan was probably a sign something about him spelled disaster.

Besides, kissing Han in the doorway before she left on her mainte-nance rounds, Leia had to admit to herself that they were happy. Han made her happy. He wasn't dumb by any stretch of the imagination, it was just that his thinking felt... Leia had trouble finding the right word. Maybe the word she was looking for was ordinary.

Later Leia looked at Han sitting on the ground surrounded by a semi-circle of children of all ages.

"*Haak* say uh *moobi*?" Han said.

The children all touched their index fingers to the tips of their noses. She couldn't deny the sight gave her a warm feeling.

"*Tsaa*," Han encouraged the kids. Behind her Olga was bored with waiting.

"Ready to go?" Olga asked, offering Leia a radiation gauge.

"Thank you, ma'am, don't mind if I do. After you." Leia gave a silly fake bow and a gesture toward the twelve o'clock radial ladder.

Still, there were things that had to be done, and they had to be done routinely, boring though they might be. Would have to continue to be done if they wanted to remain alive.

Everything seemed to be in order, but everything had to be double-checked just the same. All their lives depended on the status remaining quo.

Which was how Leia and Olga came to be staring at a seam in the hull in an off corner of Sagan's garden, and the needle on the meter on the end of the red zone.

"Why now? It was within safety limits the last seventy-six times it was inspected," Olga said.

Leia wasn't so sure. "It's a small section in an out of the way corner. Maybe somebody needs a refresher on the importance of thoroughly inspecting every single seam every single time."

"It is a pain trying to get behind all Sagan frigging plants," Olga said, inclining her head.

"The weld's faulty, it's got to be." Leia ran the meter over the seam again." We checked these back on Earth over and over again." "We have the technology, we can repair it," Olga said.

"But what about the plants?" Leia asked "the exposure can't be good for them."

Olga didn't have an answer to that, but true to her word she would fix the seam.

Between Olga and Leia, Olga was definitely the better welder of the two. Which was why she was welding a reinforcing plate cordoned off from the rest of the garden deck. Meanwhile Leia stood with her foot on the *Wet Floor* sign and talked to Sagan. Of course the floor wasn't wet, it was supporting the rope blocking off a ten foot radius around Olga.

"Any way of knowing how much damage there is?" Leia asked.

"It's mostly succulents in this area and they tend to be pretty tough. I don't have any experience with radiation though." Sagan's forehead was pleated like a fan.

It was, Leia realized, the first conversation they'd had where Sagan managed to breathe between words, probably because he was thinking about the plants. She wondered what he'd been thinking about the other times they'd spoken and didn't particularly like the hypothesis she came up with.

Big Viola, aka Grandma Viola, was Leia's Grandma Daisy's youngest sister and had been eighty-nine when they left Earth. It scared Leia half to death to think of the g-forces on her brittle old bones during lift-off. But the idea of leaving Big Viola and Uncle Harry behind scared her even more.

Whenever Big Viola sought her out, Leia felt honored. Usually Han spent more time with Big Viola than Leia did.

So when Big Viola strode up to Leia with her cane in her hand and said, "I want you to have that girl do something for me." Leia frankly delighted.

"What girl? There are a lot of girls on this ship, Auntie," Leia asked, as pleased as she was she was still confused.

"You know the one, Imelda's baby girl." Big Viola was impatient but that was her usual setting.

Apparently, Big Viola was above calling anyone else by her own name, because she couldn't mean anyone but Little Viola.

"Sure Auntie Vi, whatever you want," Leia said.

"Good, you can tell her I want her to make me a *kahne*, you know, an old time teepee out of that SCOBY stuff."

"What for?" Leia asked without thinking.

"Because I've been listening to your uncle Harry snore, and he's been pulling the covers off me in the middle of the night and elbowing me in the side of the neck for more than 65 years and I'm through. Finished. This way he can visit me for a cuddle if I feel like it and I can kick him out when he starts to get on my nerves, because I know he will sooner or later." Big Viola told Leia's chin angrily, because she was on the short side.

"Okay," Leia said, both surprised and understanding the issue completely.

Thirty sleep cycles later, Leia heard Sagan talking to Wayne, Kelly, and Amber down by the succulents.

"So do you want us to compost them or..?" Wayne asked.

"Would you throw your grandma in the dumpster if you found out she was sick?" Sagan was indignant.

"Depends on which Grandma... ow!" Wayne shrieked as Amber smacked him on the shoulder.

Kelly laughed out loud.

"Gah, you two," Amber said.

But it was true. About ten percent of the succulents were growing strangely. Some were lopsided and hollow in the center. All of them were discolored or at least colors other than green. Some were grayish purple, some blue, some brilliant red. One on the edge of the obvious damage branched outward and upward from a bowl-like center. Looking down into its surface was like gazing into a kaleidoscope with multi-colored horns curling out from the center in repeating patterns. The other ninety percent were dead.

The survivors were clearly affected. Leia didn't see how they would ever be the same again.

Little Viola's *kahne* was a hit. Big Viola loved it. And so did lots of other women. Little Viola immediately had requests for more.

Not long after, Leia's Uncle Boy, who was ten years older than Leia, and Little Martha, who was thirty, came to her while she was doing routine maintenance.

"Hey," Leia said.

"Hey," Uncle Boy said back. "You know we're out of beads, right?"

Leia didn't bother to look up. "I've only heard that about once or twice every twelve hours or so, for a couple of years."

"We were thinking we'd like to do some quill work," Uncle Boy plowed on, ignoring Leia's complaint. "Only we're out of quills."

Leia grunted in sympathy, focused on the job at hand.

"We heard there's some porcupines frozen in the ship's storage," Little Martha chimed in.

"Porcupine embryos," Leia corrected her.

"Yeah, and we thought we could turn on one of those tanks on the medical level, and grow some porcupines," Martha continued.

"Where are you going to keep 'em?" Leia asked.

"We thought we'd put them in the garden level. Let 'em run around," Little Martha said and it seemed logical to Leia.

"Talk to Sagan about it. He can help you figure it out."

Leia loved Han. The more she thought about it, the more true she knew it was. She had come to love Han. But she couldn't help but admire Sagan's quiet and thorough-mindedness, and wonder if maybe the two of them would have been a better fit. Besides... he was cute in his way. Leia knew she loved Han, but that didn't stop her from admiring Sagan from a distance as he worked on the gardening level.

Leia loved Han. That didn't stop her from chalking it up to wishful thinking and her own overactive imagination when she thought she caught Sagan looking at her.

"I think somebody is liking it for you," she muttered to Olga once Sagan had gone back to whatever he'd been doing before.

Olga laughed.

"Not me, no way. I'm sorry, I'm shallow, but no. Not if he was the last single man on the ship and he's not," Olga said "Besides, he was looking at you."

"He was not, and he's kinda cute in his way," Leia insisted.

"No, he's not. He's a nice man, a reliable man, and a smart man, but he is also a very unattractive man," Olga said.

Leia didn't know why it hurt her feelings, but it did. She also had the distinct feeling that to say one more word would give something away she needed to keep under wraps, although she wasn't completely sure what.

After her maintenance shift, but before her turn in the cockpit, Leia came back to find the kids braiding each other's hair, and Han sewing a complicated folding cloth box.

"What's that?" Leia asked, retying the tie on Castor's front braid. It was all the rage on the ship now, traditional braids for everyone. Top knots for little girls. And for boys like Castor and Pollux two braids in the back, a long skinny forelock braid hanging down artistically in front. Good thing every other parent and grandparent was willing to help out, Leia could never keep up with the maintenance.

"I'm making my brother something for his seeds and cuttings," Han said. "When it's closed it looks like a box and when he opens it there're eighty-eight pockets, see?"

"Wow, that's... uh... very cool." And it was strange because Leia felt jealous without knowing exactly who she was jealous of.

PART III

YOKO HYTES; OR HOW WE BECAME MORE OURSELVES

S ometimes Leia wondered if it was her friends and family, or if maybe the problem was humans in general and the ship hadn't been designed with the needs and behavior of homo sapiens in mind.

There were three habitation levels on the ship. Three floors that combined open spaces with individual cabins designed to house couples and individuals. And yet every person on the ship had eventually wound up living on a single floor. They could have spread out if they wanted, but they simply chose not to, repurposing the two unused levels for other uses. Leia climbed down the radial ladder to a burst of sound as Kelly and the other singers continued their song around the big pow wow drum.

If Leia designed a ship it would have only two primary levels, and each one's day would be the other's night. The lack of a day and night had affected everyone's sleep. Leia couldn't help thinking everyone would feel better if they had day and night.

Leia braced her feet on the ladder's rungs and checked the ship's interior seams with her Geiger counter.

Kelly kept right on singing.

Women who weren't on shift had on their shawls and were dancing.

A gaggle of children were running and laughing, playing chase.

"Leia!" Sagan called across the level immediately averting his eyes when she jumped off the ladder and approached him.

"There're someseedsandbulbs I'd like to bring out of storage that needacoldseasonto germinate," Sagan mumbled in that fast but quiet way of his.

"The environmental controls aren't the kind of thing I feel comfortable playing around with if they aren't broke. It's too dangerous," Leia said. "You can use the refrigerators, can't you?"

"Not really. I mean, I could but we don't really have enough room and it can be disruptive, you know? It's not really self-sustaining," Sagan was looking at the ground, covered with soil he had made.

Leia tried not to sigh, Sagan put a tremendous amount of work into building self-sustaining food forests. It was ironic, but every time she said so he responded by blinking rapidly and arguing even faster. Apparently, she was a horticultural idiot.

Her mind had been wandering when Sagan looked up and the two of them were somehow staring deeply into each other's eyes.

That wasn't what she wanted at all.

"Trying to terraform Mars is bullshit and it's a recipe for disaster if Earth sends the other two ships. It's setting us up for ready made war. We're maybe two hundred years away from what might be another habitable planet. That's too far to mess around with the system that keeps us alive. We've got to weigh our risks and…" Leia stopped, she'd run out of words and could only cough and shrug. "I've got too much on my plate already to make up something else to worry about. We're going to need water sooner or later. The filtration system works but not 100%."

Those were her words, but her heart was pounding and her panties were getting so damp you could float tiny rubber ducks in them.

Sagan bit his lower lip.

Leia leaned in closer.

And then…

And then...

Leia kissed him. His lips were soft and his breath was sweet and she loved the smell of his body.

Without warning Sagan pulled away. Everyone was looking.

"I... uh... no," Leia said, backing up three steps and coughing again. Her mouth had gone completely dry.

Everyone was still watching.

Sagan kicked the ground.

Leia turned and ran.

Sagan would never be able to give a good explanation of what happened next.

He was sitting on the ground with his head in his hands listening to the sound of his blood rushing through his ears. Eventually he looked through his fingers, and what did he see?

He saw the mutated succulent. The one Leia described was shaped like a fractal, although he personally thought it was somewhere between a deer's antlers and a snowflake. Later generations would call it the Deer-Star.

Without thinking about it or even particularly wanting to, Sagan's hand reached out to one of the tiny geometric buds.

For the rest of his life people would ask Sagan why he did what he did. All he could say was that it seemed like the thing to do at the time.

Sagan put the bud into his mouth.

Pulling back slightly, as Sagan put the bud into his mouth, eyes closed, he knocked his planting box—the one Han made him that was so keen—with his knee. It fell open like a bursting bud. The old word for a bud ready to open was the same as the one for a bus or a pregnant woman; *muraroi*. Carrying us.

Leia was still running. Leia never ran . Her side hurt and she felt like she was going to throw up. She hated cheaters. She didn't want to be a cheater. She hated liars and here she was, lying every minute she didn't tell Han. She had to tell Han. Where the hell was he anyway?

Finally, Leia reached the doorway to her room and pressed the code to unlock.

There in their room was Han... in the bed... with Buttercup covered by a sheet. Leia was grateful for that sheet.

Han looked at her with wild terror in his eyes but he clearly had prepared his speech in advance. "Is it so hard to believe I love both of you? Besides, it's traditional. In the old days when you married a girl you married her sisters," Han said defensively, covering his nipples with the sheet.

All the emotion drained out of Leia like waste water down a pipe. Her expression was as flat outside as she felt inside. She wasn't sad or guilty anymore, or even angry. She felt nothing but calm. She looked from Buttercup to Han and back again.

"I thought we were just gonna be yoko hytes but... sure... okay, if we're going to be traditional we're going to go all the way. If you're married to Jasmine and Buttercup, I get Sagan, too. Which I better because I kissed him in front of everybody up on the garden level. Now I'm gonna go to sleep with him. I say sleep but..." Leia turned to Buttercup, who hadn't said a word, and pointed straight at her a cold rage rising up out of nowhere. "And if you're going to play this game, Chuy's my husband, too now. We're just an old-fashioned traditional f amily."

Having said the words Leia felt nothing but cold air blowing through her veins again which was why it surprised her when the air around her began to throb green and aqua blue.

Han clutched harder at the sheet, the air around him strobing.

"What the..?" Han said, looking around the cabin, terrified.

"Excuse me, it looks like we have a bigger problem than this romance bullshit," Leia said and struggling to put one foot in front of the other left the cabin.

As she walked down the corridor to the ladder, she did her best to ignore all the frightened looking people, not to mention the air filled with colors, colors that pulsed like the beat of a drum. She wanted to stop and reassure the people, but no, the whole ship would be better served if Leia focused on finding out what the hell was going on. Somebody else could do the comforting.

A group of children were huddled, scared against the wall. She saw Flower and Persy among them but instead of stopping she broke into a run, the air flashing faster, a swampy green covering everything around them. Every molecule visible and vibrating.

Everything around Leia seemed to fold, to open and fold, repeatedly. Everyone around her seemed welded to the spot but Leia willed herself to keep moving. She had to get to the cockpit and figure out what was happening.

If she had been able to view the ship from the outside it would have been the same. The ship in space—everything strobing—and then the ship—gone.

Sagan struggled to fold up his planting box, but somehow his planting box was grown. Not enormous, somehow bigger than enormous. It was as if his planting box was everything.

Space, stars, planets, folded like Sagan's box with the ship inside. With a hand that was bigger than a planet, Sagan picked up the Futura and moved it from one pocket to another.

Sagan took a deep breath and, reaching more with his brain than his arms, because his arms were too short by miles, he closed the box successfully.

Olga and Amber sat in the cockpit, strapped in their seats as Leia reached the top of the ladder and the air went still. No colors. No flashing. The air, still and once again invisible.

"Holy Moses! What just happened?" Olga said.

On the monitor the stars had changed and below them was a planet. A big swirling blue and white planet. Like Earth only without the land masses. It looked to be oceans, nothing but oceans, frozen at the poles, with a layer of cotton candy clouds indicating a functional water cycle.

"O, Is that a planet????" Amber asked, "That's a planet, right?"

Leia held onto the ladder and hung her head through the doorway of the cockpit. Olga and Amber turned to look at her.

Jesus, her side hurt.

"Is that a whole planet full of water? Nothing but water? 'Cause that looks like a whole planet full of water... How the hell did we get here?" Leia gasped for breath.

Leia heard heavy steps on the ladder and stepped forward into the cockpit.

A minute later, Sagan crowded in behind her. "I think I can answer that last one. I umm. You know the mutated succulents?" he asked. "The one that looks like a little deer? The antlers anyway. I ate some. I thought I was hallucinating but I think I was folding… uh… space. Is that dumb? Does that sound as dumb to you as it does to me?"

"If the ship was still in the same place it would sound dumb," Leia said. "But seeing as we've moved so far, I don't think we have any way to chart our current position. It sounds more plausible than hallucination. Far as I know hallucinations don't move ships through space. Much less find water."

"Did I find water?" Sagan asked.

"We're not sure but you might have found a whole planet full of it. Now we just have to figure out if it's drinkable," Amber said.

Two weeks later Leia noted, after sending a probe to collect samples and analyzing the samples in every way they could collectively imagine, in the ship's log that the water was pristine. They called the planet Suma Pa'a. First Water. It would become the center point for all future star charts. It framed all future reference. A ship was either moving towards Suma Pa'a, the place the human beings first found water, or away from it.

And so it was that Sagan Sleepy-Eye became the ship's other primary pilot. The one who never entered the cockpit but instead closed himself in a small dark closet meant for janitorial supplies, because he found it worked best. And There he folded space and time around the ship until they reached their desired destination.

On his first intentional journey, he took the ship to a planet, strange and swampy. Once Chuy, Kelly, Jerome, and Tilly took four space suits and a lander down to the surface, they learned it had a breathable atmosphere. It made a kind of sense seeing how it was almost entirely covered with dense plant life more comparable to ferns than anything else. Its largest animal life were crawly things no bigger than a child's hand, something like an aardvark, something like a meatball.

They sent down a second lander manned by Buttercup, Jasmine and Leia, primarily because they were the ones who wanted to go. Unfortunately, there were some unforeseen circumstances, namely the lander not landing particularly well. What had seemed like solid ground, was like most of the planet, closer to the texture of a rotten pumpkin. The lander touched down and sank, then listed to one side. From inside the lander, the sound of metal under pressure scraped their ear drums.

Jasmine unbuckled her harness. "We should get out of—"

Leia raised her hand to stop her just as the scream and snap of a strut breaking shook the lander and everything rolled, including Jasmine.

To her credit Jasmine didn't make a sound except to say, "I think it's broken." once the lander rolled to a stop.

"It's pretty safe to say the lander is no longer in factory condition," Leia said :but we can probably...

"No, I mean my arm," Jasmine said.

"Good thing for you, you brought a nurse," Buttercup said.

Leia did not make a crack about Buttercup's past as a psychiatric nurse, even though she wanted to. She was more concerned with getting the lander in shape to carry them back to the ship.

She opened the hatch, grunting as she turned the wheel to unlock the door.

"Leia?" Buttercup called from behind her back.

"I just want to see what kind of shape we're in," she said without turning around.

Inside the lander, Jasmine was less stoic as Buttercup set her arm. Leia did her best to ignore the short sharp cry. It was one of the struts. Leia took off her helmet so she could get a better look. Not just broken but twisted too. Leia couldn't do anything about the strut on her own. She was going to need Olga's help and she was going to need a welder.

She breathed in deeply. It smelled vaguely like the log ride at the Midwest City amusement park. She wondered what kind of microbiotic nasties this planet was crawling with. Now was not the ideal time to find out.

She turned toward the hatch to tell Buttercup to keep Jasmine in the lander just in time to see Jasmine climb out, bracing her good arm against the lip of the hatch. Her bad arm hung in a blue sling

"Maybe you ought to play it safe, stay in the lander," Leia said.

"Are you kidding?" Jasmine chuckled. "And miss the chance to see a new planet? I wanna explore."

Leia sighed. She wasn't in charge, it wasn't her place to tell Jasmine or anyone else what to do. It just seemed safer to stay inside.

"Yeah, we want to see what's out here," Buttercup said, coming up behind Jasmine. "We won't do anything stupid."

The radio at Leia's waist came to life, buzzing. "You here, Wurahapt?" It was Chuy.

"We're kinda having an issue over here," Leia said, as she sank up to one knee in the mushy ground. Another of the little animals, about the size of a computer mouse, looking more like a cross between an armadillo and a kiwi fruit, spray-painted green, came out of the underbrush to look at them. Leia couldn't tell whether it had scales, armor, or feathers. Whatever they had was green though.

"Huh, look at that, will ya?" Buttercup pointed at the animal with her lips.

"I wonder what they taste like. It looks like it has some meat on it," Jasmine said. "It doesn't have any fear of humans, we could at least try one. I'd share with you."

"No way," Leia said, pulling her leg out of the mud.

"Just because you're a food wuss," Jasmine said, standing on a patch of solid ground.

"We didn't evolve on this planet. We didn't evolve to eat anything that evolved on this planet. Even if they're not outright poison there could be long term deleterious effects," Leia warned her, scraping the mud off her space suit.

"You know she's right." Buttercup agreed, folding her arms across her chest.

Jasmine laughed. "Maybe, and maybe you're both a couple of killjoys. I think they look delicious. The perfect single serving meats. You could peel them and stuff them, maybe make a little sauce *verte*."

The foliage began to shake and a familiar, cheerful face came through the green. Jerome, followed by Tilly, Kelly, and Chuy bringing up the rear.

"There ya are!" Jerome called.

Leia was grateful they showed up before her sister started fricassing the wildlife. Apparently she had managed to land closer to Landing Party One than she initially thought. The dense plant growth had obscured their location.

Leia and Olga wound up spending two weeks on the surface together repairing the lander. They named the planet Pia Payu? Yukatu, "Big Muddy." Although Leia could never mention it without adding damn or fucking for emphasis. She never went on another landing party for the rest of her life. It became policy, people who worked on the ship's systems were discouraged from joining a landing party. The risk was too high to the welfare of the ship.

Willingly restricted to the ship Leia started drawing in her free time, thinking of how she would build a generational ship from scratch if she ever had a chance. Sometimes the ideas came to her in her sleep so strong she sat straight up and scrawled it on the pad she kept at her bedside. After a while Han didn't even wake up.

Soon after that, Little Viola set to work making Leia a *kahne* of her own. For five sleep shifts, Sagan shared it with her. When she invited Chuy Alverez to spend the night, it was more as a way to help Sagan and Han to make up by giving them a common enemy than anything else.

The second time she invited him to visit her in her *kahne* it was simply because she wanted him there. She also revised her understanding of intelligence. It was possible, she realized, to be right, to understand and know things, without being able to explain how or why. She rubbed her eyes a lot these days. She figured all Sagan's plants were aggravating her allergies. Strange things, little disturbances she couldn't quite see, darted in and out of her field of vision.

For their next trip, Sagan returned the ship to Suma Pa'a, mostly to make certain he could.

It didn't take long for others to want to join him learning to fold space. Some people just couldn't do it. Others couldn't tolerate the plant's effects. Leia tried and spent 48 hours puking her guts out. She did take them to an asteroid belt made mostly from a metal harder than any alloy on Earth, non corrosive, and yet in a small window of temperature and pressure, profoundly ductile. Meaning paper thin sheets fitted to the outer hull of the ship made them a hundred times less vulnerable than they had been.

Olga named the metal whose properties she'd discovered, Emetica, after Leia's stomach problems. They called the ring of asteroids the Emetic Belt.

Leia found it an annoying joke until Emetica became so common and sought after that it was simply the word for metal plating. No one thought of the original meaning any more.

It should probably be noted Leia's ninety-six-year-old Uncle Harry was a natural at folding space.

It was Sagan, though, who first mentioned Leia's designs to anyone.

Olga was on Garden Level Wahat, doing her rotation checking radiation levels, as usual levels were unremarkable.

"Whaddayathink about Leia's designs?" Sagan asked, on his knees scrutinizing a plant.

Olga froze immediately, switching off the gauge, then in slow motion she turned to face Sagan. "What designs?"

"Her ship designs. She wakes up and works on them when she's supposed to be asleep,"

"In that case I can't tell you what I think because I've never seen them." Olga switched back on the gauge and got back to work.

Next time they were piloting the ship together Olga brought it up.

"I hear you've been holding out on me," Olga said casually, double checking their position in the asteroid belt.

Leia appeared to be genuinely puzzled.

"Sagan says you're making ship designs, too," Olga tsked vaguely.

"You, too?" Leia couldn't help herself, she laughed. "We need a real hobby."

"I know, right?" Olga joined her. "Oh, you live and work on a spaceship? Would you like a little more spaceship to go with your spaceship?"

"Maybe a spaceship mug and spaceship pajamas to wear after a long shift fixing and flying a spaceship?" Leia added.

"Only if I can wear them while I'm drawing spaceships." Olga giggled.

Outed, the two of them marked the end of every shift critiquing and improving each other's ideas. Ideas, though, were all they stayed. Life was too busy and survival too precarious and demanding during that first generation for anything else.

Olga and Leia were in the control room. Everyone who wanted to be trained to pilot the ship had been trained to pilot the ship. Since they both liked working together they regularly scheduled their shifts together. They did this with the clear understanding that one or the other or both would come running at the first hint anything was less than boring normal.

"People are talking, Lay," Olga said.

"What about?" Leia checked their trajectory, not that it mattered. If you're not going anywhere in particular it doesn't really matter which way you point your ship, given you avoid collisions.

"Things disappearing. Little things, hair medallions, beading needles. I hear Chuy lost all his socks. They're saying it's The Little People," Olga said.

"Somebody's pulling a prank," Leia reassured her.

"I'm sure you're right, but people are talking about it, saying the

Little People…" Olga went on.

"You're not supposed to talk about them too much or you'll make them show up." Leia also wanted to say she was getting uncomfortable, and she wanted not just Olga, but the entire ship to drop The Little People as a topic. However, she herself didn't feel comfortable enough talking about them to make sure everyone else stopped talking about them.

"But their name…" Olga started.

"Don't say it out loud!" Leia stopped her.

"Doesn't it mean us-Comanches somewhere in space and time?" Olga asked.

"Someone's pulling a prank is all that's happening," Leia assured her again.

Eventually, whoever it was pulled enough pranks that Leia and Olga doubled the maintenance checks in hopes of catching the joker. They didn't find a single hair tie much less the prankster.

Three babies were conceived and born before Sagan and the other pilots took the ship to what might traditionally be considered an inhabited planet.

Everyone left what they were doing to discuss it before the landers left the ship.

"I'm notevensure what inhabited means, youknow?" Sagan said. Everyone was leaning in his direction, stone silent, trying to parse what he was saying.

"You know what inhabited means," Chuy scoffed. "You know what we mean when we say it."

"You'd thinkso but…" Sagan huffed dramatically. "If there's life onaplanet it'sinhabited. Just because somethingdoesn't thinktheway-wethink doesn't mean it's not alive."

Leia didn't feel she knew enough about it to poke the topic with a ten-foot pole.Others weren't so cautious.

"A plant then," Han said.

"A plant's alive. Plants think. They have relationships," Sagan said.

Mutters of "what?" "What the hell," echoed around the habitation level. If he'd said it when they first took the ship people would have shrugged it off. But now, because they knew Sagan, knew he was so often right they had to take what he said seriously and they didn't like it

Sagan nodded, "plants communicate along mycelium networks," Wayne and Viola and others, particularly those who worked with the plants nodded along. "Mother plants channelnutrients and and and moisture totheiroffspring for years. Theyfeelpain, respond the deaths ofplantsaround them. Ifyouthinkaboutit who'stosaywe'respe-cialjustbecausewehavelanguage? "

Uncle Harry, so old he looked like he was made of wet paper sacks, laid his hand on Sagan's shoulder. "Slow down and breathe, son, say what you're trying to say."

"There. Are. Little. People. Down. There." Sagan puffed out con-sciously, pausing between each word and the next.

"Tell 'em about 'em," Uncle Harry said.

"I mean, they're not people, not human being type people anyway, but they, you know, they build houses, places to live in, and they, you know, make things." Sagan struggled to speak clearly in spite of himself. Leia wasn't worried. He was trying to be clear and everyone was doing their best to listen to him. Understand him.

"Tell 'em about the things they make," Uncle Harry said, his arm across Sagan's shoulders.

"Irrigation canal system, looks like, covering about half the planet and I think they got lawn sculptures, youknow yardart," Sagan continued.

Leia leaned against her *kahne* wondering what alien lawn ornaments looked like. She was curious but she could wait for the landing party's video stream. She wasn't that curious.

"Looks like I'm going to the surface. How about you, brother?" Chuy asked Sagan.

Sagan shook his head silently. So far, Sagan never wanted to join a landing party and no one was much interested in pressuring him to.

"Alright! I'm in," Uncle Boy said, laying down his quill work. "I'm coming, too. I gotta see this."

"Fuck, yeah!" Little Martha's little brother Jason yelled, jumping to his feet.

In the end an even dozen of them, three of Olga and Leia's newly revamped and reinforced four-person landers full, also known as a *pukka*, went to the surface.

They parked the landers a few miles away from a population center and headed out to meet some aliens. Jerome took it on himself to remind them the human beings were the aliens this time.

It hardly mattered. As soon as the landing party came in sight of the town, because the town was what it looked like, one of the inhabitants, shoulder-tall, naked, and scaled with a pale white belly, raised their staff. It looked like a spear or a short lance from some old movie. And shot at them.

The landing party had no idea what it was but it came like a ball of yellow lightning and hit Jerome in the shoulder, knocking him to the ground.

"Maybe I'm wrong but I don't like those guys," Jerome grunted as Chuy ran with Jerome slung over his shoulder like a sack of potatoes. A big sack of potatoes.

"Man, fuck those guys," Jason said running along side Chuy.

"Let me down, they hit me in the shoulder, not the leg. I can run," Jerome huffed.

"You sure?" Chuy asked.

"Yeah, I'm slowing us both down, we gotta get back to the ship," Jerome said.

"You need to get your shoulder looked at," Uncle Boy said in agreement as Chuy let Jerome down and the two set off, faster now.

"I'm thinking we need to get back to the ship and come up with a plan for taking those assholes' fire sticks," Jerome said.

"And I'm thinking we need to shut up and run until we're outta this dump," Chuy said.

In the end they made it to the landers and closed the hatch before the inhabitants caught up with them, but just barely. The fire sticks didn't even manage to scuff the finish on the Emetica hull. And as promised Jerome, Jason, and the others stole two dozen fire sticks in a night time raid

Leia and Olga figured out how to replicate the fire sticks. Then they worked out how to improve them. The finished products were kept in storage in between landing parties.

There were other peopled planets. Other landing parties. Some peopled planets were happy to meet with the human beings and trade with them. Others weren't. Raiding hostile peoples, the human beings decided, was an option, provided the peoples in question weren't too weak or pathetic to fight.

~~~

So while the first designs were made by Leia and Olga it was Persephone and Flower Array who called the meeting to put them into reality.

"I would like to welcome the newest Human Being to Yuhu Wekip, fourth child of Hukiyanny and her husbands, Castor and Pollux, and acknowledge an important moment in the history of this ship. The number of Human Beings on the Yuhu Wekip has doubled since we left Earth," Persephone said in her beautiful sparkling voice, her curly cloud-like hair bouncing as she spoke.

The people murmured their approval and several women *katatakined*, ululating enthusiastically.

Then Flower Array, like her mother, short and broad, with straight heavy hair and a flat slightly husky voice, stepped in "Since we left Earth my mother and Olga have been working on designs for a new kind of ship, one better suited to Human Beings and the way we live now. I propose the time has come to build one of those ships."

"How do you propose we build this ship? Planet-side and then find a way to launch it or are you saying we should build a whole space docking system?" Yu'no'kop'pahp, formerly known as Andy, asked.

"We've been thinking about that," Persephone said in that effervescent way of hers.

"The emetic field makes the most sense, we can both harvest ore and build in the same place," Flower Array explained.

"Sort of a shipyard in space," Chuy said as it dawned on him.

"How long will it take to build one of these ships?" Mabua'Tekwa, formerly Emmet, asked.

"We'll find out when we do it," Persephone said.

"But first we need to have a long talk, all together. I'm sure there are things we haven't thought of individually that we can figure out as a group," Flower said, making herself comfortable on the ground for a long discussion.

By the time Hukiyanny's baby was walking they were in the Emetic Belt, smelting ore for what would be the first of many ships.

PART IV

Nʉnʉ̱se Hakaniku Nanahaitahkatʉ; or How We Scattered

There was a story, Leia and Olga argued about whether or not it was true, that engineers who designed the original space shuttle boosters wanted to make them wider but were forced to narrow their design in order to ensure they could be moved by rail. The standardized distance between rails in the U.S. was four feet eight point five inches. Why? Because the U.S. rail system was set up by men trained in England and that was the distance between rails in the U.K. The reason four feet eight point five inches was the standard distance between rails in the U.K. was because the U.K. train cars were built by the same people, using the same jigs and standards used for wagons in the U.K. They used a four feet eight point five inch distance between wheels because any other gauge would break down on the ancient rutted English roads. The rutted roads were initially formed by Roman Imperial war chariots designed to exacting Imperial measure, to maintain optimum stability when pulled by two horses side by side. So if the story was true, then the solid rocket boosters were made less effective because the designers couldn't break free from choices made by the guys who designed chariots for the Roman Empire.

The same was true for time. At first they went along with the signals passively received from the Deep Space Orbiter, as the Futura was designed to do, keeping the ship perfectly synced with time on Earth. But when the ship took its first jump and found Suma Pa'a the signal blinked out.

Neither Olga nor Leia were particularly bothered. Leia because she was naturally cussed and hated leap year. Olga for more practical reasons. Years don't fit well as a measurement of time on a spaceship. Unless that ship is perpetually orbiting the Earth as it orbits the sun, solar years make for an arbitrary choice. The inhabitants of the ship formerly known as the Futura didn't even know where the Earth was any more. They hadn't known where they were in relation to the Earth for the length of time it would take for a human fetus to complete gestation times thirty three. The length of gestation seemed more relevant as a measurement than the orbit of a lost planet around a lost star. At the very least gestation was a measure of time they carried with them. They discarded the old Earth-centered measurement of time for the one they carried with them and recalibrated the ship to reflect that change.

There are a million other changes, some large, some small, when a planet dwelling people become a space faring people.

The ship hadn't been called the Futura for a long time. The name had never been officially changed, and the new name itself had begun as a joke soon after they had learned to fold space around them, but they never called the ship anything but Yuhu Wehkip, "Looking for the Fattest/Best One" any more.

Leia, now known as Wehki which translated roughly as The Searcher, wasn't grand enough to consider herself old yet, although she knew she couldn't accurately be called young by any stretch. Not even Pahara, who used to be called Tilly, was what anyone might call young. Pahara and Kutse, formerly Buttercup, were at the center of what was happening now. As the two senior human beings responsible for the health of the ship they had been the ones who confirmed that the child named Narutsai had been sexually abused, not just once but subject to ongoing sexual abuse by some adult. Wehki called everyone together to decide what was to be done.

Even without their opinion, it would have been obvious when someone, or something, unknown and unnamed raggedly tore her step-father Ona'a's ear straight off his head in the middle of the act. He had come, running, screaming, naked out from a store room one ear completely gone, skull exposed. Narutsai had been found later, clearly confused about how Ona'a had lost his ear, but not about what Ona'a had done to her. He'd done it many times before.

Now there they all were, every single ship's inhabitant, except little Narutsai and Leia's Aunt Kay, sitting on the ground or on folding chairs, trying to decide what to do with the perpetrator. Victor and Pakumutsi, Persey's two husbands, stood on either side in case he decided to bolt, not that there was anywhere to go.

"I... I... This wasn't what I wanted to happen," Ona'a, or Baby, the white husband of one of her much younger cousins, sobbed. "It's not my fault." His name used to be John. They called him "Baby" because of his tendency to whine and take offense about... everything. Although, personally, Wehki had always wished there was some Nu-munu equivalent of Tolkien's Gollum to name him after. Ona'a had denied that he had been the one who had molested the child until that very moment and now he was crying loudly. Wehki was singularly unmoved. The louder he cried, the more unmoved she was.

"Are you saying it's Narutsai's fault?" Kutse said while Pahara ground her back teeth.

Ona'a cried louder, his nose starting to run. He blew his nose with a loud honk, taking the opportunity to gauge the audience's response. "I'm not blaming the girl, of course not, but she's very sexual."

Pahara sat back in her folding chair and passed her hand over her eyes. "She's nine gestations old." Her voice loud and quavering as she struggled to keep her emotions level.

"Whaa... What are you going to do with me?" Ona'a whined.

Someone toward the back of the crowd, it sounded like Vernie, the little girl's grandmother, said "Throw him out the airlock!" Shouts of agreement rippled through the ship's inhabitants.

Wehki didn't like the idea, but it took her a minute to understand exactly why. "I hate the idea of that asshole making us all into murderers," she whispered to Olga.

"Agreed," Olga whispered back.

"I'd kill him for you," Chuy said behind her. He had turned out to be a surprisingly good husband, all things considered. From him Leia had learned you didn't have to be an intellectual to have something to add to the conversation. They might approach issues from completely different angles but most of the time, she and Chuy came to precisely the same conclusion. For thirty seconds she considered taking him up on his offer, or at least putting it to a vote. No, she couldn't do that to him. Ona'a's crime shouldn't wind up a stain on other people.

"I need help!" Ona'a shouted.

Wehki looked at him, her head cocked to one side. "Even back on Earth I don't know of anyone who knows how to fix sexual predators. But I'm pretty sure there's nobody here who knows how to make you fit to live with human beings."

Olga, who had remained Olga, because she didn't want or need any other name, stood up, white hairs coiled here and there, among the black. She stepped into the center of the circle beside Ona'a.

"I think the answer is exile," Olga said." I agree with Wehki. I don't like the idea of this asshole making us all into murderers because he isn't fit to live among human beings. But there are a limited number of human beings in the universe. I don't want to be responsible for making that number any smaller even though he's poison to everyone around him."

A rumble went through the crowd. Wehki couldn't tell if it was in agreement with Olga or not, but exile had been the way they dealt with those sorts of people in the past. And by past she meant traditionally, back on Earth, before they had been forced to assimilate. Eventually, the outcasts had banded together and formed their own group. The thought of it happening that way again worried her. Still, space was a very big place. Bigger than the Western United States at any rate. With any luck he'd die alone and die quickly.

"He's still my man," The little girl's mother, and Ona'a wife, Cynthia said defensively. The baby at her breast was holding tight to her toddler, Mutsi's, dress with one hand. "I'll be alone for the rest of my life if you send him away. What about me?" she challenged.

Olga turned to look at Cynthia, "Excuse me but he's your piece of shit," before addressing the rest of the ship. "I say we give him a lander and a little deer-star plant and tell him we never want to see him again. What happens to him after that is his own affair."

The crowd got louder.

Wehki stood up and moved to the center of the circle. "Let's put it to a vote. But before we do, I want to make it clear, whatever we decide, whatever happens, it's not because of the little girl, she didn't make this happen. If he hadn't done this to her, he would have done it to someone else. It's because of him, because of what he did and what he's going to do again the first chance he gets."

Chuy raised one hand in the air. "Who says we push him out the airlock without a suit?"

Roughly a quarter of the crowd raised their hands.

"Who says we give him a lander and tell him to go?" Olga asked and a little less than seventy-five percent of hands shot up. Wehki totally understood, she kind of wanted to vote yes to both questions herself.

"Come on, we have to get packed," Cynthia said to the child.

"No, you don't," Pahara said "You're an adult, we can't keep you from going with him, but you're not taking these kids on a lander with a pedophile. We're not letting you."

"Saabe's still nursing," Cynthia said pitifully.

Olga took the baby who had begun to wail. "There are five other nursing mothers on the ship right now. We'll work something out."

Leia knelt down and opened her arms to Mutsi. Looking up at Cynthia, she said, "There's nothing we can do to stop you from getting pregnant as soon as you're gone, but if you do, the whole universe is going to curse you if you don't keep that child safe."

"Safe? You still don't know what attacked him," Cynthia's voice was quiet but accusatory.

"Whatever it is, it is free to tear the ears off of every child molester it sees as far as I'm concerned. I'm not really worried," Wehki said with a sneer and a shrug.

Cynthia took off at a run after Ona'a.

Olga looked at Wehki as she stood, adjusting Mutsi on her hip.

"You know she's not going to take any better care of the next baby than she did Narutsai," Olga said.

Pahara shook her head. "And you know she's going to get pregnant again as soon as she can. I just felt like somebody had to say it."

Olga shook her head in agreement. "You know it's not going to make a difference, right?"

"Oh, I know," Wehki said.

"And whatever attacked him? Do you think it was the—"

"Don't say it! But whatever it was, we have no power over it either way," Wehki exhaled.

A precedent had been set. As time went on and the story was passed down as part of the history of Human Beings shared among ships, exile became the highest form of punishment. Space was a big place. In her old age, when Wehki learned the outcasts had formed their own society and built their own ships, she regretted voting to spare Ona'a's life. She regretted not listening to Chuy. Sometimes even the right decision is not free from guilt, not that Wehki knew whether she'd been right or not.

Things had changed and were continuing to change.

Only a few of the people used English words for anything. As a language, English was on its last legs. It was the same when they rendezvoused with the other ships, the new ones that had been built to accommodate the ever expanding population, built from Leia and Olga's own designs.

English was for old people.

More ships had been built; The Kwahada and The Pasiwio. Those ships had been filled and in turn more ships would be built. Ships were lost, some destroyed in accidents or in conflicts with other species. Some truly lost, the survivors, if there were any, cut off from communication with the rest of humankind. The humanoid shaped absences were seen more clearly and more frequently. They no longer seemed to be taking the trouble to hide. Then they attacked. And there was no defense against them. They attacked with their sharp little fingers but somehow could not be touched by human beings in return.

On their second attack of a ship called THE GAS GIANT, one of the Deer-Star pilots, an old man called Flare, took desperate action. Amid the panic and the screams as human beings were torn and raked by the unnamable assailants, he crawled on his hands and knees to the place where the Deer-Stars grew. Touching his hand to the Grandmother plant he thanked her for her gift and took hold of the tiniest deer-star child within reach. He focused his thoughts as he stripped the skin and spines from one barely branched lobe. With all the powers of concentration he could access he bit down on the naked lobe.

The ship began to strobe. The fighting continued as the strobing colors squeezed the ship. One desperate woman, history would record her name as Aims-True, fired a blast spear in the direction of one of the Unnamables. It took the hit and recoiled. An offended shriek went up from all the Unnamables as one by one they vanished.

Nothing the human beings had done before had any effect on the Unnamables.

"I don't understand all the details," said the Old Man called Flare "But it seems to me we've learned something about both the Unnamables and ourselves."

"Yes," said Aims-True. "It's as if our weapons have been unable to affect the Unnamables because we weren't hitting them where they actually were."

"It also means we aren't just folding space, we're slipping outside our normal plane of existence to do it."

"And when do we're in the place where the Unnamables live."

"Which is why they've never attacked us during a fold, that's where they're vulnerable,"

"We should have called them Untouchable instead of Unnamable,"

"But they aren't anymore,"

The conclusion, after a long discussion, was that the Unnamables existed between dimensions, or what Human Beings understood as between dimensions, at least. For long generations after they were referred to as The Inter-Dimensional Beings.

Stops-On-Time pressed her palm to the wall of GIVEAWAY STA-TION: YUHU WEKIP, distracted from the task at hand by the presence of history. Although the station had been repaired and added to, its purpose changed long ago, she was still on board the first ship of the Human Beings. It was sacred. Yes, of course all ships were sacred to a degree. All ships were part of the people and yet greater and more important than any individual person. Not just carrying the people like a pregnant Human Being. Not just the place of the Human Beings and part of the Human Beings like the Human Beings were part of the ship. Not just the sum total of the Human Beings, the animals, plants, air, water, skin, and mechanics of the ship.

GIVEAWAY STATION: YUHU WEKIP was in the truest sense the oldest grandmother of every Human Being who traveled the long black reach of space. Without her, none of them would exist.

Stops-On-Time pressed her cheek against the cool steel brought a thousand gestations ago from poor abused and dying Earth.

"Are you just going to stand there and let me set up all this myself?" Her sister, Works-Until-She's-Finished interrupted her, standing behind her with a wide container in her arms. It wouldn't be that hard to go around her.

"Let me breathe, will you," Stops-On-Time said.

"So we can let those other ships think we're pitiful people with nothing to give while you pet the wall?" Stays-Until-She's-Finished said.

"Just because we're a new ship doesn't mean they're judging us." Stops-On-Time said.

"You know what I heard someone say. I heard those ones from the LONG JUMPER call Mother Took-It-And-Ran 'That Lady from the NEBULA,' Not the TIGHT PLATES, the NEBULA."

Stops-On-Time shrugged. "She was born on the NEBULA."

"But she built the TIGHT PLATES," Stays-Until-She's-Finished said, obviously trying not to raise her voice.

"I don't know why you're getting so wound up about this. She knows her ship. We know her ship," Stops-On-Time said.

"I want to make sure they know it too," Stays-Until-She's-Finished said. "I want to show them our ship is as rich and generous, and as full of smart, useful people doing important things as any other ship."

"Every ship was new at one point," Stops-On-Time did not particularly care what the other ships thought. Sure the TIGHT PLATES wasn't even half-capacity now, but eventually it would be as full as any other ship. It didn't bother her.

Still, Stops-On-Time shrugged and picked up her box. It was full, just like her sister's. She hadn't been able to put on the lid on account of the mitochondrial drives piled well above the top edge of the box.

"All right, I'll go back for the rest, too." Stops-On-Time said.

Stays-Until-She's-Finished poked her in the back with something hard, probably the corner of the box she was holding.

"This is the last box," Stays-Until-She's-Finished said. "You can help set up."

"If these are the last two boxes, why are you rushing me?" Stops-On-Time asked.

Stays-Until-She's-Finished sighed loudly. "Because the Giveaway has been going two sleep cycles already and everything needs to be just right when it's TIGHT PLATES' turn. We don't want to give away our best things every which way. We want to make sure they know what we're giving them. Once they start using them, the TIGHT

PLATES is going to be up there with the LONG JUMPER."

Stops-On-Time considered the possibility and found it highly unlikely. LONG JUMPER, hundreds of gestations ago, had invented the Lander Porky—the fountain shaped sensor array every member of every landing party of Human Beings used to communicate with the ship while simultaneously collecting planet-side data. And the LONG JUMPERS were still big deals because of it. She didn't see TIGHT PLATES competing with that any time soon.

"I don't want them to underestimate what we're giving them," Stays-Until-She's-Finished said. "Come on."

Stops-On-Time didn't argue and instead trudged along with her box. There was no point doing anything else. Stays-Until-She's-Finished was just being the way she always was. Doing what she always did. Rushing along, full speed ahead, so she could sit around and wait.

"Did you get the boxes Mother Feet-Up and the others made for them? The presentation boxes?" Stops-On-Time asked.

Stays-Until-She's-Finished stopped, like a bird hitting the inside of a hull.

"Can you run back to the ship and get them?" Stays-Until-She's-Finished asked.

"Let's check to see if they don't already have them first. They might have brought them when they left the shi—" Without meaning to, Stops-On-Time found herself distracted again, studying the ancient hull of the YUHU WEKIP.

Stays-Until-She's-Finished cleared her throat.

Stops-On-Time sighed and dutifully walked on, winding her way through the maze-like old station before her sister started poking her again.

Sure enough they reached the third level of the central core full of elders visiting, teenagers flirting, crowds of children racing in circles.

There were all four of their mothers, sitting under a tree heavy with fruit on a blanket spread out on the ground. Beside them were stacks and rows of bracelets, necklaces, earrings. In front was the biggest mound of all, an edifice made of boxes designed for their highest value gift. Each one individually crafted, decorated as exquisitely as the people of TIGHT PLATES' had the power to make them, an equal number in each ship's colors.

Stays-Until-She's-Finished set her box down carefully, even though it wasn't necessary.

"Well," Stays-Until-She's-Finished said looking around.

"Well, what?" Stops-On-Time asked, squinting.

"The mitochondrial drives aren't going to jump in the boxes all by themselves," Stay's-Until-She's-Finished said.

Mother Brings-Two-Blasters stood up, Stops-On-Time and Stays-Until-She's-Finished's two babies in her arms.

"And you two can nurse them while we do it," Mother Brings-Two-Blasters said, holding out Stops-On-Time's Doll-Boy, who grabbed her immediately by the head and made her look him in the face.

Stays-Until-She's-Finished took Vastness, just barely younger than Doll-Boy, who latched on easily and silently, the way Vastness always did. Doll-Boy, in comparison, pulled her nipple out of his mouth every few seconds to laugh at what the adults were doing.

Now that all the mitochondrial drives had been completed, there would be more time for babies. Time to spend with the babies you had. Time to get pregnant again. If she knew Stays-Until-She's-Finished, her sister was planning to populate the ship all by herself. At least that would be Stops-On-Time's assumption, until her sister presented her with a breeding schedule.

Still Stops-On-Time knew her sister wasn't wrong. Doll-Boy and

Vastness were both boys, so some day when they were grown they would get married and join another ship. It was the only way. There were more boy babies than girls on The Tight Plates and the ship could not grow and thrive without more daughters. Stops-On-Time consoled herself with the hope that at least one of them might be some flavor of two-spirit that would allow them to stay with their homeship. But she knew she shouldn't get her hopes too high.

"I know we've all been having a great time eating, and visiting, and flirting," The amplified voice of Sheltered-Son, a senior warrior from Long Jumper, reverberated off the walls. "But our next ship has been waiting very patiently for their turn."

Sheltered-Son switched off his amplifier and went back to his place in the audience. Their time would come soon enough. If not today, then tomorrow. He personally led the landing party that acquired ten ship weights of Emetica hullskin plating on IX. He was untroubled. He knew the worth of The Long Jumper's gift. He knew his own contribution to that gift. While no human ship was dispensable, The Longer Jumper had an established reputation for being a benefit to every human being that crossed her path. Quite similarly Sheltered-Son had proven his value among the warriors of The Long Jumper. He intended to savor the Give Away. When the time came to present their hullskin plating, humbly, of course, he would look at the ground with the faintest of faint smiles, beaming in his heart like a supernova. No one had to say a word. He knew what he'd done. They knew what he'd done. He'd done what was needed.

But before any of that happened he was looking forward to seeing what The Tight Plates had to give. They were such a new ship, it was a surprise to see them step forward at the Big Give Away. He could only assume they had come up with something very interesting. His first granddaughter had recently been born. Maybe there would be some pretty thing for her, and the thought of that delighted him. Maybe the ponds on their ship grew especially soft or colorful cloth. The thought of it delighted him.

"Where's my seat?" Sheltered-Son asked.

"Here." His brother, Red-Dwarf, handed him an unopened chair, expecting him to shake it open himself.

Very well. Sheltered-Son was nothing if not humble. He wasn't above shaking open his own chair.

Mid-wave, however, Took-It-And-Ran switched on her oldest husband, Full-Belly's amplifier and he started talking.

"My fellow human beings, we're honored to be here among you all and more honored still to be able to offer a gift, small and simple such as we have, to all of you."

Sheltered-Son threw himself carelessly in his seat, there was a squeak. One of his grandsons' toys was wedged in the corner. He reached behind himself to pull it out as Full-Belly droned on. It was stuck in there pretty tight. Full-Belly was not a dynamic speaker.

"It was during this catastrophe that my daughters, Stops-On-Time and Stays-Until-She's-Finished, came up with a new way to power TIGHT PLATES internal systems. We call it the Mitochondrial Drive. The ship's internal systems are powered using the same bodies that power every Human Being's cells. We have found that through regular drumming and singing the mitochondrial drive can be kept synchronized with its human family."

Sheltered-Son's mouth hung open. His mind boggled at the leap TIGHT PLATES had taken. Their name would be legend now.

"We have plenty of drives here for all of you to take some for your related ships as well as yourselves. The engineers of the TIGHT PLATES have opened our systems panels and are ready and waiting to give demonstrations and help any interested with their installation."

Sheltered-Son was happy for the TIGHT PLATES. He wasn't a bad guy. He just wished the TIGHT PLATES hadn't outshone the LONG JUMPER during his lifetime.

"Run, baby, run, here's your chance," Grandmother Rides-Rough shuddered out the words, pinned under a fallen tree. "Take my deer-star-child."

The girl named Utility-Belt ran grabbing the plant hidden inside her Grandmother's sleeping cone, her scrawny dog, Blacky, following close behind. Blacky had to be scrawny, or when times were tough someone would have eaten her. Still, she was fast.

Another blast shook the ship, and all the inertial dampeners in the universe couldn't keep Utility-Belt from skidding across the dirt floor of the ship. Struggling to keep the pot with a small deer-star-child safe and upright, tearing her knee open in the process. She didn't bother to try to wipe it clean as she pulled herself to her feet, and took off again heading for the central hatch of the ship. Blood trickled cold down her leg, mixed with grit and soil. Her fingers sore, she unscrewed the door to the daytime side of the ship. Blacky jumped down the hole ahead of her. Utility-Belt reached for the first step toward the central docking drum of the ship as another shot rocked the ground under her feet. The girl felt her bare foot lose purchase on the first rung of the descending ladder. Her free hand grasped at nothing as the ship rang like a bell.

Instinctively Utility-Belt drew her knees to her chest and rolled, protecting the plant with her body. She hit the floor of the central drum with a bone jarring thud without losing momentum, or her sweaty grip on the deer-star-child, her backbone rebounding against the wall. Not bothering to pause to get her bearing, Utility-Belt raised herself to her feet and continued her race to the launch bay as the ship shook around her. But she couldn't stop, not if she wanted to get away before her father made her his next wife.

Her single-minded goal finally achieved; she didn't come to a stop until she slammed her busted knee against the interior of the Little Pukka Lander. Blacky licked half-heartedly trying to staunch the blood from her leg. Ignoring her pet as she struggled to her feet, Utility-Belt wiped her palms on her dress and fired the thrusters, trying to get free of the moorings with her other hand, fighting to remember everything her grandmother had told her about piloting a ship.

She fired again, this time breaking the Pukka loose with a grinding roar. Thrusters on maximum, little Utility-Belt leaned every gram of her scanty body weight against the console, breathing hard as she piloted the ship away from the two warring vessels with no place to go and no place to hide. The Pukka's plating shuddered with every blast the ships sent at each other. She had no idea who would win. As always Utility-Belt's home-ship was bigger, much bigger, than their opponent. But as usual the other ship was more maneuverable and in obviously better shape.

Utility-Belt didn't know what to do. She could not, would not go back.

Since she could remember, her grandmother, Rides-Rough, had told her life was different on other ships, and when they were alone they talked about the day they would make their escape. While no one disputed the fact that her grandmother had been stolen from another ship when she was a young woman, still, her mother said her grandmother was "a crazy old woman" and men were the same everywhere. Life was the same everywhere. Much as Utility-Belt loved and wanted to believe Rides-Rough, all she knew was the ship where she was born. What was she supposed to do?

Rides-Rough had told her as soon as they found another human ship they could signal it and find safety. All they would need to say was that they had escaped from the Rotten-Crotches.

There was no arguing that Utility-Belt's people weren't called the Rotten-Crotches. There was no disputing the fact they didn't fight other human ships every time they encountered them either. But if she went to the other ship for shelter would it really be any different from the ship where she was born? Was there any guarantee she would be treated any better than the females on board her home-ship? She found it hard to imagine. And if life was different for females there, did she have any guarantee they would win the battle against her homeship?

"What are you going to do?" Blacky asked her.

Utility-Belt blinked repeatedly because well… Blacky had never said anything to her before and she hadn't expected her to.

"I don't know," Utility-Belt said. "Why are you talking to me? Dogs don't talk."

"Because I'm not a dog," Blacky said. "Look at me."

Utility-Belt looked at Blacky. She didn't know why she had never really looked at her before, she was her dog after all. Or she thought she was her dog. Except now that Utility-Belt looked at Blacky, she realized it was not an easy thing to do. Every time she tried to focus on Blacky, Utility-Belt's brain fought against her eyes' effort to make sense of what exactly she saw. All she could make out was a lack of color, a lack of light, and an overpowering urge to look away.

"I can't look at you. Why didn't I ever notice that before? What are you?" Utility-Belt asked.

"I think you have bigger problems than me not being a dog," Blacky said as a near miss sent the Pukka swinging end-over-end.

Utility-Belt screwed up her courage and worked the controls to hail the attacking ship as it tipped and dodged fire from her home-ship.

Across the Pukka, Blacky observed her coolly.

Three things happened more or less simultaneously.

Utility-Belt found her voice and said to the enemy-human-ship. "This is the Pukka Lander Stands-Alone. I have escaped from the Rotten-Crotches and request shelter."

Utility-Belt's home-ship's fire struck the enemy-humans' pilot-side thrusters and the ship came tumbling toward her.

Then, worst of all but most expected, Utility-Belt's home-ship and the human-enemy ship fired directly at her, or maybe they fired at each other without caring that she and the Pukka were in between them.

In a moment of sheer panic, the young girl took a bud from the deer-star-child and jammed it into her mouth. A spine pierced her tongue as she tried to imagine her Pukka on the other side of the nearest star. She knew of nowhere else to go. There had to be some way to hide from the home-ship's sensors.

As her terror grew, she jammed more and more of the plant into her mouth, despite the fact that Rides-Rough had told her one small bite only. Utility-Belt went on eating even as her mouth filled up with blood. There had to be some place to hide. Some place where the photons wouldn't reveal her location. Not knowing what else to do, she ate the rest of the plant, even the root. She'd never heard of anyone eating the root before. It had two legs like a Human Being. All Utility-Belt wanted was to disappear.

Blacky made a short sharp sound high in her throat somewhere between a bark and a laugh.

Utility-Belt didn't have enough words, or the right words, at least, to describe the place where the deer-star-child took her.

"Where is this? Where are we?" Utility-Belt asked the being she used to think was her dog.

"We haven't gone anywhere," Blacky told her.

"But everything is different," Utility-Belt said.

And it was true, there was no sight, no light, but objects and motion continued to exist in Utility-Belt's mind. That is to say she perceived beings and objects and motion by means she had no language to describe and in fact was struggling to process. Through these senses Blacky came into sharp relief, a being of her own size and shape and relative density. What was more, she was one of three. Three humming, popping, fizzing beings who were also, somehow, girls like her.

"What are you?" Utility-Belt asked again.

"In one sense, I'm your dog, Blacky," the little being made of snaps and pops and humming electrons said. "In another sense, I'm you yourself. In another, you might say I'm your daughter. You might say we're all your daughters."

"I don't understand," Utility-Belt said.

"Take my hand and you will," said one of the girls, but two of the three extended their small hands to her, palms up, fingers splayed, linking their free hands with those of their other companion.

Not sure what else she could do, Utility-Belt took what was offered to her.

What happened next started at her palms, the awareness that she herself was just like the three girls who made the rest of the circle, made of fizzes and snaps. They were the same. Like singers at the same drum, the pops and vibrations that made up the tips of Utility-Belt's fingers started to fire at the same time as the pops and vibrations in the fingertips of the girls whose palms pressed against hers.

Like a stream running across the floor of a ship, the shared rhythm raced through the four little bodies. And as their electrons vibrated in harmony, so did their thoughts.

Utility-Belt understood now. When, in her pain and panic, she had eaten enough of the deer-star-child to kill her a dozen times over, choked to death on her own blood and vomit, her tongue pierced full of needles, somehow she had moved, not the Pukka but herself. But the movement had not been through space and time but beyond both. Moved was the right word but it was also the wrong one. There had been movement involved but instead of using movement, she became movement. She became what the other girls called Dark. A state beyond the reach of sight or any of the humans abilities to perceive directly.

The four hearts beat in unison. The four brains crackled with electricity burning in a complex web between them. Not just the four of them but a vast network of them spreading across the cosmos. A web of millions.

Each was a separate individual and yet somehow not...

Both a single child and an entire species, as matured as they would ever be. Like one song sung in countless variations rising to a powerful chorus.

When the girls released Utility-Belt's hands, there were eight of them.

They nodded at each other, vibrations rippling across space. They were in agreement. Both ships had fired at her.

"You're right," said the girl who had been her dog, Blacky. "Humans are the enemy."

PART V

RELATIVISTIC JET AND THE MARTIAN; OR HOW WE TURNED AROUND AND MET OURSELVES

R elativistic-Jet sat halfway up the number four radial ladder at the map room end of the ship watching two of his mothers corner a porcupine. Just a dozen more rungs up and gravity would be loosened enough that he could let go of the ladder and move on his own through the loose-g to the map room if he felt like it. But not yet. A dozen more rungs would also make the difference between being able to see what his mothers were doing well enough to be entertained by them and Primes-The-Thrusters and Strips-Wires-With-Her-Teeth turning into two tiny moving dots.

Below, on the central drum of the ship, Strips-Wires-With-Her-Teeth charged the porcupine and Primes-The-Thrusters threw the blanket in her hands. But from the movement of their bodies, he could tell the porky had escaped, run through the berry thicket on the other side of the old pecan tree.

But he knew his mothers. Neither of them were the kind to give up. Eventually they would get the blanket over the porcupine and walk away with his old baby blanket full of quills. These they would clip the barbed ends off of, dye, soak, flatten, and sooner or later use to embroider his name, Relativistic-Jet, on something he owned. And if they didn't write Relativistic-Jet they would settle for a visual depiction, a flare of particles escaping from the event horizon of a black hole. It was kind of a mania with all six of his mothers lately. They were all constantly making him new clothes, jewelry, tools, weapons all emblazoned with his symbol. Even his new atomizer gun had the design, which looked like a ray piercing a flattened disc, inlaid in precious stones on the butt. It was a very nice, brand-new atomizer and the symbol looked very striking but it was also a little bit embarrassing. When was too much too much?

It was both exciting and terrifying to think about the reason they were doing this. Soon, in less than a standard measure, the length of time it took a human being baby to grow inside the body and emerge alive, they would rendezvous with another ship of human beings and if Relativistic-Jet met a woman he liked, a woman who also liked him, he could tell his mothers and they would arrange a match. His first-mother, boss-wife Extinguishes-The-Fire, gave him her word none of them would make a match without his consent.

He thought about the upcoming meet-up with another ship. He would be lying if he didn't admit to some pangs at the knowledge that once a match was made he would be leaving his family behind and never return to his home-ship except as a visitor.

But that was the way of things.

Oh, from time to time, if a ship was getting too crowded or there was some kind of long-running insurmountable conflict within a ship, a group of sisters might build their own ship. But most of the time women stayed on the ship where they were born. Which was why girls were taught to tend to business inside the ship from the time they were little. It would be their responsibility to keep the ship running, make sure there was air to breathe and water to drink, make sure the plants and animals were thriving and the gravity kept them affixed to the central drum. Make sure the thrusters were firing so the ship could be maneuvered. Keep the *Puuku*, the four person ships used for setting down on a planet, in good shape.

It was Men's Work to make the maps and use those maps along with the Deer-Star-Plant to move the ship through space. It was Men's Work to sing and drum at the mark of every sleeping and waking, to remind the heart of the ship to beat, and to keep the hearts of the people and the heart of the ship synchronized with each other. It was Men's Work, alongside the Women Warriors, to defend the ship. It was Men's Work to protect the landing party, so that women could decide what, if anything, a planet might have that the Human Beings might need. Then it was the job of the men to get it for them. Whether by charm, or by negotiation, or trade, or, as a last resort for obvious practical reasons, by simply taking what they wanted and running as fast and as far as they could.

The Women's job was to run things inside the ship while Men were expected to handle things outside the ship. His fathers and grandfathers had put time and effort into preparing him to be a man, and needless to say to attract the attention of women. He knew how to let his looks speak for themselves.

He had already proven he knew how to keep calm in a fight. He was a good shot with his atomizer, but his real strong suit were his powers of persuasion. He was also very naturally good looking, but he wasn't going to say that out loud. He shouldn't have to. It was obvious.

Not that plain, or even ugly boys, couldn't marry well but... every little bit made a difference. Didn't it?

He figured he ought to be able to make a good match, though he went back and forth in his mind over whether it would be better to have an older, more established well-experienced wife with several husbands and co-wives or whether he would prefer to begin a new family branch in a first-husband/first-wife type situation. He had turned the thought over and over, and approached it from every angle he could find but he wasn't sure.

His reverie was broken by his sister, Walks-In-The-Vacuum, below him on the ladder, dressed in her space suit, shouting at him through the suit's speaker. Four more of his sisters, each in their own space suits, with their names and the ship's name, The Star Shield, painted on the chests, stood lined up behind her.

"Relativistic-Jet, I know you're too pretty to work but could you at least get out of the way so other people can get their chores done?" Walks-In-The-Vacuum said, her voice undistorted through the speaker.

Walks-In-The-Vacuum was stubborn, but he could be stubborn too, when he felt like it. Something about Walks-In-The-Vacuum always made him feel like it.

"Go back down. Use another ladder," he said. "I'm sitting here."

"We're half-way up. We're not going to turn around, go back down, then go all the way up another ladder just because you decided to get in the way," Walks-In-The-Vacuum said.

He had fully intended to go talk to Great Grandpa Whisper in the map room. The trouble was Walks-In-The-Vacuum spent so much time telling him not only what to do but also how to do it, when to start, and when to stop. He couldn't help himself, he looked Walks-In-The-Vacuum rudely in the eye, folded his arms against his chest, and said "I think I'll stay right here," hooking his feet on the rung below him.

"We're doing this for you, and you won't even get out of our way," Forward-Momentum, at the rear of the line of sisters, but a head taller than the rest of them, said with disgust.

"How are you doing this for me? Did they tell you to paint my name on the side of the ship?" He asked, almost serious.

It was Walks-In-The-Vacuum who answered, "You probably think we ought to, you vain thing. But no, we're touching up the paint on the hull so your future in-laws don't talk bad about the shape your home ship is in. Otherwise they'll bring up that raggedy paint job every time you do something dumb," she gestured for him to go up the ladder, because she was tired of waiting.

In response he leaned back and settled in.

The next thing he knew Walks-In-The-Vacuum gave him a short sharp jerk of her head and the rest of his sisters; Reinforces-The-Hull, Avoids-Work, Counts-The-People, and Forward-Momentum, shimmied up the sides of the ladder. Grabbing him by his arms and legs, they heaved him, one... two... three... four out of their way. He was tossed with all their considerable communal strength... not down, no, they wouldn't do that... but up where the gravity was light and after a split second of surprise he bounded away slowly, laughing.

Oh well, he meant to visit Great Grandpa Whisper in the map room anyway.

"Thanks for the boost," he shouted at Walks-In-The-Vacuum, shaking his buttocks in her general direction. Then he took one, two, three leaps forward and propelled himself in the direction of the very tip of the ship's map-side cone. Landing feet first at the door flap to the map room, he met the inner hull plating with a soft thud, his bare toes gripping the plating as he righted himself and knocked at the wall beside the flap.

"Great Grandpa Whisper?" he called. "It's me, Relativistic-Jet, can I visit? Are you busy?"

Instead of Great Grandpa Whisper, his best friend, Hytes, answered the door.

"Not busy at all my boy, come on in, come on in. Make your report," Great Grandpa Whisper called behind Hytes' shoulder. Great Grandpa Whisper was a very small, very round Human Being, but his voice was extremely deep and commanding. Great Grandpa Whisper waved from the other side of the map room. It turned out he hadn't been as close as he had sounded. The map room could be tricky like that. Great Grandpa Whisper was on the far side of the map and had the Mother Deer-Star-Plant floating beside him.

"You tell it. What do you have the Big Mother for?" Jet asked, because it was strange and the mothers and grandmothers didn't like you to take plants into micro-gravity.

"Oh, I'm just having a talk with my friend here," Great Grandpa Whisper said almost quietly. "I'll have her back before your Great Grandmothers find out."

Great Grandpa Whisper made friends out of everyone. It was what made him such an excellent trader. He cared what you needed, whether he knew you or not, and it was not an affectation. And if it was in his power to get it for you, even if you had nothing to offer him in return, he would make it happen. It seemed like everyone in the galaxy knew Great Grandpa Whisper and owed him… something.

That was how Hytes had joined the ship. It happened before Jet was born but everyone, even on other ships, knew the story.

It had started on the planet Igcks. The people of Igcks considered dance the highest of all art forms and once a solar cycle, they held a contest and the prize was three hundred weight of high-quality ship metal.

Now it was a fact that Human Beings did not evolve in space. In order to keep their bodies fit for landing parties, every day, every Human Being danced as soon as they could stand. In addition, there were daily games, foot races, women's ball game-played with a large leather ball and no hands, men's ball game—played with sticks and a small ball, but every Human Being was at least a good dancer. Not bragging, just stating the facts.

It was also a fact that while Great Grandpa Whisper had always

been a short round man, he was well known to be the greatest dancer
in all the ships of the Human Beings. Again, it was a simple fact.

And so it was that Great Grandpa Whisper danced on Igcks and
won the grand prize of three hundred weight of valuable ship metal. However, amid the festive atmosphere of being awarded Igcks's
highest honor, Great Grandpa Whisper crossed paths with a wretched
creature chained to a rock in front of the home of a prominent citizen.

Great Grandpa Whisper asked, as anyone would, what this person
had done, what crime they had committed.

The Igcks explained, very amused with the great dancer, that this
was no person, but a wild Beast, a lower animal who had been captured
in the countryside as an infant when the rest of its band had been
killed for thieving fruit from orchards on the outskirts of the city. The
prominent citizen looked on it as if it were one of his own children,
or at least that was what The Igcks told The Human Beings. His
owner even supplied the Beast with mildly narcotic herbs, which the
wild Beast rolled into a tight cylinder of leaves, put to its mouth and
inhaled. The herbs kept the Beast complacent and happy, the chains
kept the Igcks safe from the Beast's barbaric nature.

Great Grandpa Whisper observed the Being chained to the rock.
The Igcks indulged the honored dancer's eccentricity and carefully
prevented him from coming within reach of the Beast on his tether.

He could simply go on and leave the Beast as he was, chained to the
rock, but the longer Great Grandpa Whisper stood there the less that
option sat comfortably on him.

Great Grandpa Whisper could have decided to simply take the
Beast and race, as quickly as possible, back to the four-person lander.
The trouble was Great Grandpa Whisper wanted to maintain good
relations with the Igcks. It was in the best interest of the ship and

any other Human Beings that came to Igcks. Besides, Great Grandpa Whisper liked the recognition he got dancing on Igcks.

In the end, Great Grandpa Whisper did the only thing he felt he could do, under the circumstances. He traded three hundred weight of ship building metal, enough to replate half the ship if you rolled it thin enough, for the freedom of the chained Beast who had no name.

Great Grandma Fills-Her-Collection-Bag laughed and shook her head when Great Grandpa Whisper tried to set The Beast loose, but The Beast refused freedom, preferring to follow their party back to the lander. Great Grandpa Whisper rode back to the ship with The Beast on his lap, even though it was almost twice Great Grandpa Whisper's size. Great Grandma Scans-The-Planet was so mad about what her husband Whisper had done she moved her private cone away from his other wives, facing the opening in the opposite direction and denying Great Grandpa Whisper entry.

The ship quickly grew accustomed to the Beast's ways, referring to him as "Whisper's Male Friend" and then simply "Friend", a name he was still called by, or "Hytes" in the language of Human Beings. Hytes was good to have at your side in a battle, whether the fighting was ship-to-ship or hand-to-hand, even though Relativistic-Jet had never seen him use the impressive fangs that hung past his jaw. Hytes never learned to speak. After scans, it was discovered he did not have the anatomy for more than panting or growls. He did learn to use the map room to navigate, and eventually to make use of the thrusters to pilot the ship in regular space. Despite repeated attempts, he never learned to use the Deer-Star-Plant to fold space. It was as if the Deer-Star-Plant simply refused him communion with the minds of the ship's other elders. Hytes never had forsaken the habit of his youth and continued rolling any leaves he could find into cylinders so he could breathe in the smoke, which he was doing now, floating in the almost complete weightlessness of the map room with Great Grandpa Whisper, the tip of the cylinder glowing as he floated, rings of smoke coming from his snout.

"Did you come to talk about getting married, my boy?" Great Grandpa Whisper asked.

A shiver raced across Relativistic-Jet's skin. How did Great Grandpa Whisper know? He always knew.

"Don't look so surprised, I been alive one hundred forty gestations, my boy. I got the whole universe at my fingertips and I still spend most of my time thinking about women," Great Grandpa Whisper laughed. "Besides, your time is coming, everything's about to change for you, becoming a full grown man, going to another ship. If I was you, that's all I would be able to think about."

"But how do I choose? I mean what if I pick the wrong one? What if I marry one girl but then I meet someone better on a different ship? If I leave, won't her whole ship be mad at me? And will my new wife ever really be able to trust me?" Relativistic-Jet said. A strange tickling sensation on his back. He looked over his shoulder at Hytes who shrugged. Maybe the topic was making him sweat.

"You never really know until you've been with 'em for... five... maybe six gestations minimum," Great Grandpa Whisper said, searching the star maps that covered the wall of the round room.

"But what about the rendezvous?" Jet asked, the odd feeling had moved down the back of his breech-cloth and he squirmed.

"Them girls sneaking into your mothers' cone to sleep with you is a damn good time and all but tryin' each other out isn't the same as being married. Not at all," Great Grandpa Whisper said as he floated gently around the room. The Deer-Star-Mother floated beside him.

"How do I pick the right one? How do I know? " he asked as Great Grandpa Whisper slowly rotated his finger tracing a trail of stars on the wall of the little round room.

"Well that depends..." Great Grandpa Whisper started, but Jet lost the rest with the realization that the burning end of Hytes's leaves had floated into the back of his breech-cloth.

Against Relativistic-Jet's will, he yowled and flailed against the microgravity, fighting to put out the burning embers trapped between his buttocks and testicles. His arms flailed. His legs paddled in different directions at the same time. Without meaning to at all, Relativistic-Jet smacked Great Grandpa Whisper in the back and sent him spinning headfirst into the Deer-Star-Mother. He was stabbed by a pang of shame that was cut off by the continued burning in his breech-cloth.

The ties.

Jet needed to release the ties on his breech-cloth. Burning and spinning, he fumbled to untie his breech-cloth and get the embers away from his most precious and consequently most tender parts.

Panicked fingers caught the tie just as the walls began to pulsate, glowing green and purple, blue and orange. Space began to contract, he himself folding helplessly and down into his own center, smaller and smaller, until space and the ship and everyone on it were concentrated down to a single point of pink-black light.

Either an eternity or an instant passed by and all things, himself included, began to blossom outwards.

By the time space had stopped pulsing and unfolded everyone back to their right sizes again, the ship had moved and Relativistic floated naked in the map room, his breech-cloth in his hand, a scorched circle in the center. The ship was eerily silent.

Great Grandpa Whisper turned around, his face marked by two clear rows of the Deer Star Mother's protective needles sticking out of his cheeks.

"Hear That?" Great Grandpa Whisper said, raising his chin and narrowing his eyes. "The heart's stopped."

The heart of the ship was not beating. It was the first time in Jet's life he had been in a completely silent ship. He strained to listen. In the distance, coming from the edge of the ship's gravity, he could hear the chirping of birds but that was all.

Great Grandpa Whisper and Hytes were already diving towards the door flap.

"My sisters are outside," Jet said the words as he thought them, then repeated them louder in case Great Grandpa Whisper hadn't heard. "My sisters are outside!"

"Well bring 'em in," Great Grandpa Whisper said. "I gotta go see if we can get the ship's heart beating again."

Jet nodded, moving, as if in his sleep, to the flap.

"And put your breech-cloth back on," Great Grandpa Whisper called over his shoulder as he climbed onto Hytes' back for the quickest ride possible down to the central drum of the ship.

Don't panic, it won't do any good. Relativistic-Jet reminded himself, tamping down his terror at what he'd done as he re-tied the strings of his breechcloth, wondering if the singed center would hold. He exited the map room flap and swam with the longest steadiest strokes he was capable of toward the air-lock. Grasping the red hand-holds beside the first air-lock seal, he came to an abrupt stop and pressed the intercom.

"Are you out there? Hey! Sisters? There's been an accident... an, uhh, unforeseen occurrence. Something happened. Are you okay? Are you there?" he asked the speaker.

He waited for the count of eight and hit the flip switch again, already impatient.

"Make your report. Sisters. Are you there? There's been an accident. I repeat, make your report," he said, his lips almost touching the speaker.

He was about to start making his way down the ladder to get his own suit and search for them when a voice came crisply over the speaker.

"We'd respond quicker if you'd let us get a word in edgewise," said Forward-Momentum.

"Sorry," he said. "Are you okay??"

There was a hesitation, as if they didn't know how to answer the question.

"We'll be in as soon as we retrieve Walks-In-The-Vacuum's suit."

Her Suit?

The thought stunned him. Something in his chest felt cold. He floated for what felt like a long time at the air-lock until with a dry hiss, the doors to air-lock number one opened then banged to a close once his sisters were safely inside. He watched on the screen as the doors to air-lock two sucked open and his sisters moved to the second airlock, followed by the heavy clang of metal on metal.

Down below, at the central drum of the ship, a low beat sounded, chased after by another and another and then a series of rapid bounces, synchronizing the drummers on the pilot side of the ship with those on the map side. He breathed in sharply as the singers began to sing. Beneath the voices and the drums the ship herself remained silent.

On the screen, the four sisters were eerily purposeful, no playing around as they moved through the third airlock and into the fourth. Walks-In-The-Vacuum's suit hung slack over Forward-Momentum's shoulder.

What happened to Walks-In-The-Vacuum?

As much as the two argued, Relativistic-Jet loved his sister, maybe more than any of the others. Maybe that was why they argued.

Faintly, like a baby's snore, Jet felt a thrumming begin hesitantly in the inner workings of the ship. It was thready and faltering but the ship's heart was beating again.

Jet's own heart clenched as the pause between beats lasted longer than it should have then restarted a second time slowly growing stronger.

He had no option but to be aware as the ship's systems, the human beings, the plants and animals on board came back into rhythm just as the fifth and final air-lock opened its lips and his sisters emerged.

"What happened?" Avoids-Work asked.

He opened his mouth, struggled to put the accident into words, closed his mouth and considered his choices, opened his mouth again. "Great Grandpa Whisper had the Deer-Star-Mother up in the map-room."

Forward-Momentum and the others glared at him in a way that let him know they were pretty sure that whatever happened had been Jet's fault.

"Hytes dropped the fire off his rolled-up leaves," Jet admitted, pausing in shame. "down the back of my breech-cloth."

"We need to get down," Counts-The-People said.

Reinforces-The-Hull just shook her head.

Relativistic-Jet dove out of the way, meekly following his sisters down the number eight radial ladder. The five of them climbed down, leaving behind their usual laughter and insults wherever they had lost Walks-In-The-Vacuum. As they descended to the drum of the ship, the singing grew and expanded to full force like the blooming of a flower or a child being born. Still the ship's pulse beat only weakly through the interior plating.

Forward-Momentum reached the drum first, her boots hitting the dirt and Walks-In-The-Vacuum's suit swinging over her shoulder like a sack. One by one, the sisters jumped to the ground followed, finally, by Relativistic-Jet himself.

Jet was shocked to see not only Hytes and Great Grandpa Whisper, but Great Grandpa Structural Beam, who had been dead half of Jet's life.

"Where's Walks-In-The-Vacuum?" Great Grandpa Whisper asked.

"We don't know," Forward-Momentum said, removing her helmet. "Her suit was empty when we finished folding."

As if to make her point, she threw the suit down onto the ground. An instant later, Walks-in-The-Vacuum's suit began wiggling violently. The sisters jumped back, frightened. But Great Grandpa Whisper and Great Grandpa Structural-Beam leaned close pulling free the locks on the suit's helmet.

In a matter of moments a tiny figure, by Relativistic-Jet's estimation, roughly 1/10th Walks-In-The-Vacuum's original size, climbed out of Walks-In-The-Vacuum space suit shouting in a high squeaky voice. "Couldn't reach the microphone all of a sudden."

"I'm sorry, My Girl," Great Grandpa Whisper said. "There was an accident."

"What are you sorry about? Is that what made you all so big?" asked Walks-In-The-Vacuum, apparently unphased.

"We're not big, you're little," said Forward-Momentum, almost bending double to address Walks-In-The-Vacuum.

"It's my fault, I had an accident in the map-room with the Deer-Star-Mother," said Great Grandpa Whisper, rows of spines still sticking out of his checks.

"What was she doing up there?" Walks-In-The-Vacuum asked, only the curled corner of her mouth showing how hard it was for her to hold back the interdimensional-level bawling out she would have blasted at anyone else. Relativistic-Jet couldn't help himself, he was staring at her in fascination. Jet could tell she was on the verge of upbraiding him as a safe target when she looked over his head at Great Grandpa Structural-Beam. "You're dead," she said.

"I was dead. I'm not any more. Whisper called me back," Great Grandpa Structural-Beam said.

"What's it like?" she asked, her voice now like a tiny glass bell.

"Did you ever have a beautiful dream that started to evaporate as soon as you opened your eyes?" Great Grandpa Structural-Beam said, signing the word *e*vaporate for emphasis.

Walks-In-The-Vacuum nodded but looked unsatisfied.

"So what did you call me back for anyway?" Great Grandpa Structural-Beam said turning to Great Grandpa Whisper.

Great Grandpa Whisper sucked his teeth uncomfortably "I didn't intend to. I was just talking to the Deer-Star-Mother and thinking about when we were young men and used to talk about finding the home world and how unfortunate it was neither one of us was probably going to see it. Seems like balance would be served if we could go back to the place we evolved."

"Are things out of balance now?" asked Avoids-Work.

"I would say balance is more of an ongoing process than a static state," Great Grandpa Structural-Beam said, "a verb not a noun."

Great Grandpa Whisper shrugged. "Maybe it was all *eshaap*... Maybe it was just a passing fancy, wondering if there are any human beings left there."

"We've been twenty-seven thousand gestations in space, maybe it's time to go back," Great Grandpa Structural-Beam said, tucking the wooly hair that escaped back into his braid and looking at Relativistic-Jet out of the corner of his eye. "Not to stay so much as to just take a look around, see if they got any good looking Earth girls."

Relativistic-Jet had to remind himself that the elders couldn't read his mind, it only seemed that way because they had been around a long time and were very, very smart.

"What about me? Why did you do this to me?" Walks-In-The-Vacuum asked plaintively.

"It was balance. Sorry. I was thinking about balance and how the ones with the biggest will have the smallest bodies," Great Grandpa Whisper said.

Walks-In-The-Vacuum folded her arms smugly across her chest and looked around the map-side cone of the ship. "Do you think you really brought us to Earth?"

"Only one way to find out," Great Grandpa Structural-Beam said.

"Yeah, We got to go to the pilot room. Look at the scans," Great Grandpa Whisper nodded.

The sisters, the two Great Grandfathers, Hytes, and Jet prepared to descend to the other side of the ship, where it was night instead of day, and where, from the very tip of the opposite cone, the ship was piloted. Forward-Momentum and Jet slowed their pace to match Walks-In-The-Vacuum's shortened stride.

However, they were interrupted by two heads popping up through the hatch.

Old Man Alive, who was the oldest man on the pilot-side of the ship but not nearly as old as Great Grandpa Whisper or Great Grandpa Structural beam, and Great Grandma Scans-The-Surface were followed quickly by Great Grandma Fills-Her-Collection-Bag.

"Where have you brought us?" Great Grandma Fills-Her-Collection-Bag asked.

"And why didn't anybody tell us we were folding?" asked Great Grandma Scans-The-Surface.

"It's got people on it. Real live human beings," said Old Man Alive.

"I didn't mean to, but it's Earth. I was thinking about Earth when I did it," Great Grandpa Whisper said defensively. "There was an accident with the Deer-Star-Mother."

"Is she all right?" Old Man Alive asked.

"I took a small bite. That was it," Great Grandpa Whisper said. "And it was an accident."

As far as Relativistic-Jet knew, no one ever ate a ship's Deer-Star-Mother. They only ever used her children, the tiny buds that appeared at her sides, to fold, and even that in very small amounts.

The Great Grandmothers looked at each other.

"It's not Earth anyway," Great Grandma Scans-The-Surface said. "It's the fourth planet in the system, not the third."

"We need to go talk to the others," Walks-In-The-Vacuum said.

Great Grandmother Scans-The-Surface and Great Grandmother Fills-Her-Collection-Bag looked at each other and then at Great Grandpa Whisper.

"Yes... I did that too," Great Grandpa Whisper said, peevishly.

"And he brought me back," Great Grandpa Structural-Beam said, stepping forward.

Both old women threw their arms around Great Grandpa Structural-Beam, squeezing him tight.

"Thanks for getting me out of trouble, brother," Great Grandpa Whisper muttered.

"Anytime," Great Grandpa Structural-Beam whispered back.

A look of far off concentration fixed Great Grandpa Whisper's features. "You know, I think this might be Mars."

"Sobeesu," Old Lady Remains-At-The-Helm said to mark the beginning of formal storytelling.

The Human Beings from both sides of the ship had gathered together and were sitting on their collapsible chairs, listening to her story. Though the pilot-side inhabitants were still rubbing their eyes from being awakened in the middle of their sleep cycle, all attention was concentrated on the single point that was the oldest woman on the ship.

"Four hundred thousand, maybe five hundred thousand years ago, Human Beings evolved on a planet called Earth. And for a long time they were content. They lived on their home world. They lived in hardship sometimes. Other times they lived in ease. But they respected the system they lived in, it never occurred to them to do otherwise," Old Lady Remains-At-The-Helm said, pausing for the tale to sink in.

The people of The Star Shield nodded in thought, even though it was a story everyone had heard multiple times, a story that had been carried in the data storage of every ship in the fleet since the first recorded voyage, recorded in both standard Human Being and the ancient language of English.

"Then a few certain human beings had an idea, they thought they could ignore the life cycle, disregard the ecosystem they depended on, separate themselves from the other animals and plants, take more than could be replaced, not only in their lifetime but in a hundred lifetimes. They ruined the air and the water and the soil. Soon whole nations sank in the rising seas. Rains dried up. Food withered in the fields. Soil blew away and dust choked out the sun. In a short time, the climate was unsuitable for human beings," Old Lady Remains-At-The-Helm said.

Hytes, who had heard the story at least as many times as Jet had, was crouching low, focusing on what Remains-At-The-Helm said but fidgeting, scratching absently at the dirt with his fore-claws like he wished he had some herbs to burn, but was too ashamed to light up, considering the events in the map-room.

"So the very ones who changed the climate decided to leave Earth. They were just forty families but they controlled most of the resources and had all of the power. They commissioned three ships to be built, primitive ships, but that was all they needed for their plan to begin again on the fourth planet in the system, Mars."

Relativistic-Jet considered the possibility that their ship was now just beyond the orbit of Mars.

"The ships were only intended for the forty families, but an engineer who was never meant to be one of those who started again on a new world filled one of those ships with all the people she loved the most and she stole that ship. According to the laws of the times, she and her two sisters had settler names; Leia, Buttercup, and Jasmine, but they were really called She-Searches, Stand-Up-And-Be-Strong, and She-Scares-People. She-Searches was an engineer. Stand-Up-And-Be-Strong was a healer. She-Scares-People was a cook and a gardener. Together with their friends and families, the three sisters were the founders of all the fleet of Human Beings, as numerous as the stars in the sky." Old Lady Remains-At-The-Helm looked around at the assembled people.

"Old Lady Scans-The-Surface, Old Lady Fills-Her-Collection-Bag, Old Man Alive, The Returned Old Man Structural-Beam and I have discussed recent happenings and we have come to the conclusion that Old Man Whisper and Hytes have brought us back to the home system and we are now outside the orbit of Mars," Old Lady Remains-At-The-Helm said. "Scans confirm surface inhabited by permanent settlements of human beings."

A wave of astonished muttering rippled through the crowd.

"I don't even know how they decided they wanted us to get Martian children. I mean 'One for every family on the ship?'" Relativistic-Jet's brother-in-law, Dimensional-Buoy, said, stowing his gear under his seat in the puuku.

Jet hadn't said a word himself, but he did wish he had been there to at least hear how the Grandmothers and Great Grandmothers had come to that decision.

"Diversity is health," said Jet's second father, Exploder, doing the standard triple check of the puuku's systems as the others; Avoids-Work's two husbands, Dimensional-Buoy and Ion-Trail, and Relativistic-Jet strapped themselves in.

The Ship had moved out of visual range of the planet's surface. Now twenty five puuku landers were leaving the Star Shield in hopes of making a stealth landing on the nightside of the planet's surface without the Martians noticing.

"Don't we always say there are as many human beings as there are stars in the sky? Why do we need more?" Dimensional-Buoy asked.

He would complain about anything, but this time it seemed to Jet that he might be just a little bit right. People were the most important resource on a ship though, and more genetically different people would always be valuable.

"Yes," Exploder said, adjusting the ship's energy net. "And every one of those human beings is descended from the two hundred fifty-three who left in that first stolen ship. Our lines haven't crossed with the Martians in a thousand generations."

"What I don't understand is why we don't try to make a trade first?" Ion-Trail said, settling into his seat.

It was true. Human Beings gave away the best children, exchanging the cleverest and the prettiest regularly between ships. It was a good way to maintain ties and keep the genes fresh, everyone agreed. Relativistic-Jet himself had been a gift from a ship called The Water Finder, not that he remembered it.

Of course it was sad for the parents, but also a source of pride. Besides everyone knew children grew up badly if you were stingy with them.

"We don't even know how to speak to them," Exploder said. "Besides, to be perfectly honest, they don't even have the ability to travel in their own solar system. There's not much they can do once we leave the surface with the children. Launch one of their handful of clumsy nuclear weapons? If they manage to hit us with one of those, we deserve to die."

"Why don't they have space travel? If their ancestors left Earth at the same time as ours, in the same kinds of ships, shouldn't they have the same things we do?" Jet said as the thought occurred to him.

Exploder smiled. "That's the difference between planet-side cultures and spacefaring people. If we lost enough redundant systems to lose our history, we'd be dead in space. But planet-side cultures rise and fall, and lose everything, and start over again all the time. When we left Earth, known human history was only six thousand years old, but human beings had been on Earth four hundred thousand years at least."

"So we could have gone to space a dozen times before?" Ion-Trail asked.

"Could be," Exploder said with a shrug extending a small compact to Dimensional-Buoy. "Now it's time to stop second-guessing people who've forgot a heap more than we'll ever know and go over the plan again, but first put this on your skin, anywhere it's visible."

"Why?" Dimensional-Buoy asked, even as he took the cream and rubbed it dutifully into his skin, because he was Dimensional-Buoy.

"You haven't seen the visuals," Exploder said with a broad grin calling up an intimate view of the habitation zone.

Sure enough, there were human beings scurrying back and forth down busy streets. They seemed to favor a variety of fanciful and colorful hats. Their skins were all within a very narrow range of variations of the color brown.

"The Great Grandmothers say our ancestors came in many colors, too, but Sarah on the first ship carried a mutation for a harmless variety of what the ancients called methemoglobinemia that passed through to their descendants, and we're those descendants," Exploder said with a laugh.

Without a word, Dimensional-Buoy handed Relativistic-Jet the compact full of cream.

Jet looked down at his fore-arm as he laid down the first swipe of paint. It was strange to think of Human Beings being any color other than blue.

The puukus set down as silently as leaves in perfect fractal formation outside the Martian habitable zone. It was not Jet's first raid, but he had never stolen a human being before.

Of course, Relativistic-Jet had fought before. He had fought Turners, Slipstreamers, and the inexplicable beings who intruded from other dimensions impossible to look at directly. He once even fought, hand-to-hand, another Human Being boy just a few years older than himself from another ship. Maybe that was the problem, among Human Beings the conflict was always personal. Taking the Martian children was definitely personal, but they were not going about it in a personal way. The way they were going about it was an act of war.

And yet these were fellow Human Beings.

As Jet exited the puuku, he asked himself if this was a statement or a question and he could not answer.

He was excited and yet a sense of shame pulled in the area of his solar plexus. Martians; human beings like them, and yet not like them.

"The building where the children are housed is forty *kahne* that way," Exploder said, pointing with his lips.

And like that they all jumped on their surface-runners and fell in formation behind Exploder. Together they were an even one hundred. On their surface-runners they were a swarm.

As they approached their destination, Relativistic-Jet understood the danger of what they were doing in his belly. The Martians didn't seem to live in towns or cities but in a giant continuous belt around their planet's equator. At the edge of the habitable zone, the buildings were like apathetic faces, shut tight, but nothing on Mars was isolated. Between the shuttered buildings were piles of garbage, also shuttered, wadded balls of refuse. Their scanners said there were people inside the garbage, sleeping, spotted here and there among the sleepers were some dead. Without their landing gear they would have been cold too. And if they weren't quick and silent, they could just as easily be dead as well.

Relativistic-Jet arrived close enough to the front of the party to feel the vibration of his first father, White Dwarf, opening the door with his sonic-pry. It was a tool for routine ship maintenance, but had its uses planet-side as well. Jet reached the doorway in time to see a young husband who had not joined the ship a full measure ago, his name was Time-Dilation, atomize two Martians at the highest setting. With a hiss and a flare from his gun, first one then another dissolved into fine particles. The tiny pieces blew out in all directions, the way they always did before settling out into the street. There were too many warriors behind Jet for him to do anything but keep moving.

Jet wiped the Martian dust from his face shield.

On all sides, there were warriors rushing past, keeping to the plan, taking the blanket folded across their shoulder, wrapping a Martian child securely, and running back to their surface-runners. Jet attempted to do the same. The trouble was the children were all chained in place.

White Dwarf applied his sonic-pry to the head of the shackles and they broke and fell as one.

Relativistic-Jet returned to the child he had tried to take before, threw them over his shoulder, there was no struggle.

Jet knew it was foolish at the time, there would be plenty of chances to analyze later, but he could not stop staring, trying to understand. The children behaved as though they were still chained. The children barely made a noise, and none tried to escape, instead they all stood at a moving belt, while machinery roared. The children were forming brightly colored shapes in some sort of mold, popping them out of the mold and then setting them on the belt. The shapes were then picked up by the next child and dipped in paint followed by shiny powder. They looked at what they were doing and didn't stop even when the child beside them was taken.

"There are more in the next room. I think they're asleep," Exploder said to someone behind Jet.

As Jet pivoted to return to his surface-runner he saw something.

Across the large room he saw one lone child who had not stayed at the machine. They were smaller than the others. Their hands and face coated with red sparkles and they crouched low, nearly concealed by two drums of paint as tall as a man. Relativistic-Jet was strong.

These children were thin and obviously poorly fed. He could carry two. He would take this child as well. Otherwise they would be left behind.

Jet passed the great machine now running without its little workers and the long looping belt piled high with whatever it was the children were making. Near the wall he saw a little red hand peek out between the drums. The child came forward just enough to babble something at Jet. Jet extended his hand. The child looked up into Jet's face, terror freezing its expression. He could have grabbed it, forced it to come, but he didn't want to have to do that. Jet thought of Great Grandpa Whisper and opened wide his arms.

It could have been an important moment between the two of them, Relativistic-Jet gaining the child's trust but a shout to Jet's right distracted him, the child darted away and a Martian, a grown one, with a stick at his side and what looked like a primitive atomizer barreled toward Jet.

Several high powered projectiles whirred from the primitive atomizer narrowly missing Jet's head but hitting one of the drums and raining down a shower of paint. Jet was knocked to one side. He rolled with the force that struck him, slipping his own atomizer out of its holster in the same motion. The Martian stood over Jet and his weapon in Jet's face. Jet pulled the trigger dispersing the Martian and his projectile's atoms in an aerosol mist.

Jet checked himself. He had not been hit. Why then had he been thrown? Jet looked at the child in his arms. They had been hit. The child had lived and died without making a sound.

The child who had been hiding raced toward Jet now, dripping red from head to toe. It took Jet an instant to realize it was paint. Jet scrambled for the bloody blanket that had fallen to the floor and wrapped the child tight, jumping awkwardly to his feet and making his way out the door and to his surface-runner.

They'd attracted the attention of more Martians now. A dozen or so of them, male and female, raggedly dressed stood across the road under a light, watching as they ran to their surface-runners. One took a primitive weapon like the one that had exploded the paint and fired straight up into the air. They ignored it and sped back to their puuku.

"What was that?" Dimensional-Buoy asked as soon as the puuku achieved liftoff, "Where are their families?"

"They were making... things... to put on hats, decorations, I think. Remember those hats all the Martians were wearing when we watched them on the surveillance screen?" Ion-Trail said.

Exploder grimaced. "According to what Grandma Scans-The-Surface and the others say, they figured some Martians send their children to work and others throw them away."

Relativistic-Jet looked to the bench where the other Martian children were shivering in their blankets. He couldn't set down the child in his arms even if he wanted to. It was clinging to him like Great Grandpa Whisper clung to Hytes' back. Jet didn't particularly want to set it down either.

Jet rubbed his little Martian's shaved head as the puuku entered the landing bay.

"I don't want to give him up. I want to keep him, for my son," Jet said to his mother Strips-Wire-With-Her-Teeth as he stood with her in the reclamation room peeling his Martian's paint soaked clothes off of him.

Even where the paint hadn't touched him the Martian was in no way clean. To tell the truth, he was crusty.

Relativistic-Jet's little brother, Victor, was holding a sonic-micro-pry with one hand and his nose with the other.

"If you care about him you can't be stingy with him. You don't want him to turn out bad," Victor said, handing Jet the sonic micro-pry in exchange for the Martian's paint-covered clothes. "Here."

Jet started with his Martian's toes, vibrating off dead skin and dirt. He wiggled, laughing. Sonic micro-pries always tickled, unless they didn't.

"Your brother's right. Don't get me wrong, I'll talk to Grandma Scans-The-Surface about you keeping him." Strips-Wires-With-Her-Teeth said. "But I don't want you cryin' around here belly achin' if she says he needs to go to someone else. Understand me?"

"Yes, Ma'am," Jet answered because he knew what was good for him.

"When we met your first ship I was so heart-broken because our husband, Neutrino, died, killed in an accident with his puuku. I could have laid down and died myself. But The Water Finder was dead in space and I helped your birth-mother get the thrusters firing again," Strips-Wires-With-Her-Teeth said.

Relativistic-Jet nodded but couldn't find any words worth adding.

"They were good engineers, don't get me wrong, they just didn't have the parts they needed to repair themselves. Sometimes you can make do, but sometimes, if you don't have the parts, you don't have the parts," Strips-Wires-With-Her-Teeth went on as if he'd disagreed or found fault in some way, he hadn't.

"I had no idea she was going to give you to me until we were leaving. She put you in my arms as I was going to return to the Star Shield. And you know what? She saved my life just as sure we saved theirs. I know you already love your Martian, but somebody else may need him more than you," Strips-Wires-With-Her-Teeth said.

"I had a thought, know what you ought to call him?" Victor said. "Smart-Enough, because he was the only one smart enough to run when his chain came off."

Smart-Enough, the former Martian, howled with laughter as the sonic micro-pry hit his ribs.

"I like it too, little guy. Smart-Enough is a good name," Relativistic-Jet told him.

———

That night, Smart-Enough slept beside Relativistic-Jet in Strips-Wires-With-Her-Teeth's cone. All night long the two held hands.

———

It was still dark on the map side of the ship when the alert came that they had reached Earth. Suddenly there was the pounding of running feet and Relativistic-Jet's little brother, Victor, who habitually slept in Great Grandma Scans-The-Surface's cone, came running and beat on the outside of their mother's cone with the flat of both hands excitedly.

Normally, Relativistic-Jet would have been up like he was blasted out of bed, but Smart-Enough had been jabbing him with his sharp little knees and elbows all night. Jet wondered if Martians were naturally pointier or had more knees or something. It was like sleeping with a bag full of wiggling snakes and sticks.

"We're there. We're at Earth and there are Human Beings but they're not like the Martians and they're... they're hailing us!" Victor shouted excitedly.

"What?" Jet sat up, Smart-Enough didn't wake-up, only clung tighter to Jet in his sleep.

Across the cone in her cocoon of blankets, Strips-Wires-With-Her-Teeth opened one eye. "For true?"

"They're on all the screens," Victor said through the cone's membrane. "Wake up and see for yourself."

Slower than normal, because he had to keep hold of Smart-Enough while he did it, Relativistic-Jet got to his feet and headed out of the cone. He didn't have to go far because images of Earth filled the big screen that lit up half the sky inside the ship. It was a beautiful blue and green planet. Looking at the home planet of the human beings made his skin tingle and the tiny hairs on his arms stand up. It looked like paradise.

The Earth. The first home of their species.

A transmission interrupted the beautiful blue planet with a cascade of images; a teeming city, glowing softly in the dark phase of the planetary cycle. That image was followed by a close-up of three elders with their arms open wide, which was followed by a pile of laughing children wrestling on a rug then a return to the welcoming elders and the location of the city on a coordinate grid of the planet.

"Where are the elders at?" Relativistic-Jet asked Victor, adjusting Smart-Enough on his hip.

Victor pointed with his lips toward Great Grandma Scans-The-Surface standing with her back against the Old Pecan tree. Beside her stood Old Man Alive, Great Grandpa Structural Beam, Great Grandpa Whisper, Heights, Great Grandma Fills-Her-Collection-Bag, and Old Lady Remains-At-The-Helm. They were all talking quietly amongst themselves.

Already, the warriors were gathering a few feet away wondering if the transmission could be trusted. Relativistic-Jet was with them, still holding Smart-Enough.

"It looks... believable to me. I think it's an honest invitation. I trust them," Relativistic-Jet's father, Exploder said.

"Of course you want to believe they mean it, we all want to believe they mean it, but... I don't believe it!" Relativistic-Jet's father White-Dwarf said.

"What if it's not in earnest? What if it's a trap?" an older pilot-side warrior named Trigger-Finger asked.

"If we go down there in peace and they want to kill us, they're going to kill us, we're just one ship, they're a whole planet," Time-Dilation said.

"If we send warriors down there looking for a fight, we know for sure that's what we're going to get," Avoids-Work said. She was probably right.

"Why would they want to fight us?" Gravitational-Constant asked.

"Maybe they're like the Martians and they do things that don't make any sense. Maybe we're the only rational ones," Binary-Star said.

"I'm not scared of those Earthers," Dimensional-Buoy said, which probably meant he was scared of those Earthers.

Great Grandfather Structural-Beam cleared his throat. "You're all part way right which means you're the rest of the way wrong. We've sent a transmission to the nearest ships, they are heading this way, pretty soon everyone will know. But either way, the Human Beings here on Earth have a lot more to gain from getting along with us than they do from fighting us."

Great Grandpa Whisper took up where Great Grandpa Structural-Beam had left off. "We're gonna send some of you warriors down first, and we're going to send you armed, but we're gonna send you with the best gifts we have to offer." Raising his voice to a boom, he continued, "We want everybody to find the best gifts you can come up with to share with these people down on Earth. Remember, these are the descendants of the ones our ancestors left behind, broken-hearted that they were never going to see them again. So now we're reunited, we should show them how glad we are to see them and how well we've done for ourselves."

It had been twenty thousand circuits of Earth, the home planet of the Human Beings, around its star. And now they were returning.

The Elders had decided to treat the momentous reunion with the world where they had evolved like a long awaited rendezvous with another ship.

And like that, all the people who had been milling around, debating war with our fellow human beings, went to their cones to go find an impressive gift to give to these people of Earth.

Everyone but Relativistic-Jet.

"I want to go down to the surface. I want to be part of the first landing party," Jet said while Smart-Enough drooled, asleep again on his shoulder.

"If you can get that boy to stay with anyone else," said Great Grandma Fills-Her-Collection-Bag "the sooner he learns to let go of you, the better."

Smart-Enough didn't make it easy, but in the end Relativistic-Jet went. Jet was the youngest by far of the two dozen warriors chosen to accompany Great Grandpa Structural-Beam, Great Grandpa Whisper, and Old Man Alive to the surface.

The city that contacted them happened to be pointed away from its star when they landed, so despite the warm season the air was cool and crisp. Personally Relativistic-Jet halfway wished they had worn more clothes. However, he and his mothers spent enough time getting him ready, just like the rest of the warriors, that Jet knew he couldn't look any better than he looked at that moment. His hair was braided tightly. His two lower braids were wrapped in a red cloth from Liros IV that shimmered and changed shades as he moved and made constant reports to his scanners. His scalp lock was shot through with pink metal wires maintaining contact with the ship. His make-up accentuated his best features. He had rubbed his chest and arms with an unguent that made his muscles stand out and smelled of cedar trees. His necklaces, bracelets, and earrings were all perfectly coordinated. He was immaculate, but then so was everyone. They had been gone more than twenty-seven thousand gestational cycles, it was important they looked their best when they finally returned.

The city, Chaco, was beautiful. The lands were crowded with Earthers there on the edge of the city when their puuku landed, waiting to greet them, more Human Beings in one location than any of the crew from the Star Shield had ever seen. Like the Martians, the Earthers were brown. Unlike the Martians they had the technology not only to identify The Star Shield before they reached orbit, but to hail them, and to attempt communication. Like The Star Shield's crew they were all dressed beautifully.

Their first act was to give each Human Being a bound sheaf of paper leaves detailing, in images, a gestural language. The Star Shield's crew would later learn it was the form of communication used between different nations on Earth.

Slowly, leafing through the pages in order to express himself clearly, Great Grandpa Structural-Beam, being the oldest, presented the Elders of Earth the first gift; A hundred weight of plating metal from the other side of the galaxy.

The Elders of Earth nodded and the corners of their mouths curled upward.

Beautiful women with muscles in their arms like ropes and silver bracelets came forward with trays of a hot brown foamy drink that was more delicious than anything anyone on the Star Shield had ever tasted.

Great Grandpa Whisper, as second oldest, presented his gift of The Deer-Star-Mother, although it took a long time for him to explain what she was, and what the gift meant. Relativistic-Jet wondered if the Earth Humans understood it was a gift not just to the Earth Humans but to The Deer-Star-Mother herself, who had reunited the strains of Human Beings. Even now the men of the Star Shield were grooming the Deer-Star-Mother's smartest healthiest daughters to take her place. The most cunning among them would guide the ship for generations.

The Beautiful Earth women returned with delicious cakes of meal.

One-by-one the warriors of the Star Shield made their gifts. Each gift was followed by a delicious food or drink from the Earth people.

Meanwhile Relativistic-Jet was battling an impending sense of doom. He had been so busy getting ready, so busy trying to convince Smart-Enough to stay with Victor and Strips-Wires-With-Her-Teeth, so busy trying to figure out how to convince the Elders to let him keep Smart-Enough he had no gift. That was unacceptable. What could he possibly do to remedy the situation?

In the seconds before all attention turned to Jet as the last member of the landing party to give his gift a sense of peace settled over Relativistic-Jet as the solution to his problems occurred to him all at once.

Relativistic-Jet thumbed through the papers to express his meaning, and when the time came Jet said the words as he stiffly signed them.

"My gift is myself and my son." There was no way the Elders could give Smart-Enough to someone else if they had both already been given to the Earth Humans. "All our skills, all our gifts, all ourselves will become part of you, part of what you are."

No one from the Star Shield said a word but a murmur went through the giant crowd of Earth Humans.

After a string of heartbeats, Great Grandpa Whisper leaned over and whispered in Relativistic-Jet's ear, "You sure about this, boy?"

Jet did a brief calculation, two billion inhabitants, even accounting for women too old or too young or too uninterested for consideration, still left him with far more possibilities than he would ever have rendezvousing with other ships.

"They have plenty of women," Relativistic-Jet said out of the corner of his mouth. "And Smart-Enough is a lot of work and needs at least one mother."

"It's bound to be an adventure. I give you that," Great Grandpa Structural-Beam said.

Suddenly, out of nowhere, Great Grandpa Whisper pivoted on one heel shouting out into the shadows.

"Come out, Utility-Belt, I see you over there, girl… you know what I mean. I can feel you over there. Come out and rejoin the rest of your family. We're not your enemy. Let us prove it to you."

Something began to advance. What it was Relativistic-Jet's eyes could see but his brain could not process.

ABOUT THE AUTHOR

Weyodi OldBear was born on the shores of Long Island Sound among her father's people but raised among her mother's people, The Comanche Nation of Oklahoma, where she is an enrolled voting citizen. Her work includes the Nebula nominated table-top role playing game Coyote & Crow. She is winner of the 2017 Imagining Indigenous Futurisms Award for her story "Red Lessons." Other work includes contributions to the anthologies "A Howl" and the Water Protectors Legal Collective Anthology Guide.

OTHER TITLES CURRENTLY AVAILABLE
AND ON PRE-ORDER FROM

Science Fiction & Fantasy Punks

www.android-press.com

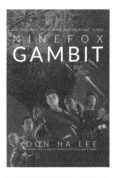

Milton Keynes UK
Ingram Content Group UK Ltd.
UKHW051602280924
448939UK00010BA/119

9 781958 121894